CHECKED

Boston Terriers Hockey #1

JACOB CHANCE

CHAPTER ONE

Tenley

AUGUST

Leaning back against the bar, I sip my wine and glance around the poolside wedding reception. My friend just married the man of her dreams and I can't even land a date with a decent guy. Smiling faces surround me while couples dance closely and contentedly in each other's arms. Romance fills the air and I'm standing here drowning my sorrows, contemplating my love life. Or should I say lack thereof?

I haven't gone on a date in three months. That's quite a dry spell for a twenty-one-year-old woman. The guy who took me out must have had a change of heart. He was completely into me for weeks, and in the span of two hours his behavior did a sudden one-eighty. He went from flirting madly to thrusting me in the friend zone so fast I got whiplash. To this day, I still wonder what happened.

Was it something I said? Or something I did?

Fuck me. My thoughts are beginning to sound like a cheesy eighties rock ballad.

Turning around, I set my wine glass down and lean my

forearms on the bar while I stare out at the beautiful northern Virginia sunset. Painting the sky with vivid slashes of orange, pink, and gold, it's breathtaking, making it difficult to feel down when there's so much beauty surrounding me. And the gentle whisper of the evening breeze wafting over my bare shoulders feels like a reassuring caress.

Relax. Loosen up. That's what I imagine it's saying to me.

I don't want to be a killjoy on this happy occasion. It's not that I'm jealous when people find their happily ever after, like my friend Jane did. She and her new husband are perfect for each other. The two of them belong together and I want her to have nothing but the best. I just wish I had some viable dating options on the horizon, so I could feel better about my own romantic future. I'd even be satisfied if something would happen to give me hope that I won't be alone forever.

Send me a sign, universe. I'm ready.

A tan, masculine forearm lands on the bar next to mine.

Damn that was quick. Is this my sign?

My eyes wander along the muscular, veined length, stopping when they reach the neatly rolled up shirtsleeves. Turning my head, my gaze continues the trek up his crisp, white, fitted shirt. Snug around his flexed bicep, I wonder if he has any tattoos under that material?

A broad shoulder caps it off so nicely, I'm afraid to look any higher. Whoever this is standing next to me, there's no way his face can possibly measure up to the rest of him. Why ruin perfection?

Curiosity wins out, though.

Oh well, here goes nothing.

His thick neck is tanned a golden brown and his sculpted lips are twisted into a derisive smirk telling me he's aware of my thorough perusal. The higher my eyes climb, the faster my heart gallops.

Oh shit.

I know those lips.

I recognize that sexy smirk.

Please be wrong.

Sweeping my gaze up, I connect with roguish hazel orbs. Fuck me. Of all times for me to be right.

Clancy Wilde, my best friend's cousin, is next to me in the flesh... in his very sexy, two percent body fat flesh.

I let out a gasp before I can hold the sound in.

He chuckles deeply, making my stomach toss turbulently, like rough water on the high seas.

"Something wrong, Tenley?" he questions knowingly. Fuck me. Unfortunately, he's aware I've always harbored a huge crush on him.

Licking my dry lips, I pray my voice still works. "Not a thing." I aim a tight, close-lipped smile his way and pluck my wine glass from the bar. Tipping it back, I drink down the remainder in one long gulp. One hand raises signaling for the bartender before the other can place the empty glass down.

He sniggers, as if he knows the reason for my discomfort, and my need for more wine. But is it really a secret? He makes me feel off balance and flushed, unlike my usual confident self.

What girl wouldn't be uncomfortable in this situation?

It feels so grade school that he knows I think he's ridiculously hot. But I'm pretty sure every girl in the free world feels that way about him.

"Wine?" he arches a dark blond brow and tips his head toward my glass.

"What about it?"

"I just never imagined you as a wine drinker."

Turning to face him, I lean my arm on the bar and prop my chin on my palm. "What have you imagined me drinking then?" I can't wait to hear this one.

"Something with a little more kick, a little more fire. It

needs to have a hint of sour and plenty of sweet. Something that mimics your personality."

He thinks I'm fiery and sweet?

"I'm your cousin's best friend. You live in Boston and I'm in Washington D.C. We've probably seen each other a total of ten times over the years. How strange is it that you think of me at all?"

"Ten times? You've been counting, Tenley?"

Fucker.

"You wish," I sass back. I take another sip of my wine, cooling down the heat that being in his company always brings.

Clancy Wilde is my most-embarrassing secret. A frequent topic in my high school journal, I recorded all the cringe worthy facts about him with my favorite purple pen in looping handwriting and i's dotted with hearts.

Thank God he's never read the entries or knows of their existence. I've no doubt he'd love to see his name at the top of my 'wish list' of guys I'd like to be with. It's a short list, but he's still in the top spot.

"Say I'm going to go along with your theory about my drink, what would you suggest?" Gripping the stem, I hold out my empty glass.

His fingers close around the rim, sliding it across the bar while his eyes study me carefully. Raking his teeth over his bottom lip, the action calls my attention to their full shape. He probably did that on purpose.

Returning my focus upward, I catch his amused expression. Yep. He did. The bastard.

"Devil's Advocate."

"Is that the name of the drink, or are you playing one?"

He smiles. "That's the name of the drink. Although, that's also one of my favorite parts to play."

Okay, I'll go along with your game. "What's in it?"

"Fireball whiskey, spiced rum, apple schnapps, and lemon-lime soda."

I wrinkle my nose. "That sounds horrible."

"I figured you wouldn't try it."

"What's that supposed to mean?"

"Nothing." He shrugs. "It's just that this drink is probably too much for you to handle."

I rise to my full height and narrow my eyes at him. "I can handle more than you could imagine, buddy."

He grins and looks at me appraisingly. "Can you now? I'd like to see exactly how much you can handle."

Wait a minute.

Is he still talking about this drink? Or is he flirting with me?

My stomach tumbles madly at the thought of him being interested in me.

Turning, I raise my hand signaling the bartender once more. He ambles over, but before I can order, Clancy beats me to it.

"Can I get a Devil's Advocate for her and a Jameson neat for me?"

"Sure thing," he replies, before moving toward the clean glasses.

"Have you ever tried this drink?" I ask, crossing my arms over my chest.

"I have, actually. One of my cousins went to bartending school and I helped him out by trying all the drinks he made."

"I'm sure that was a real hardship for you." I roll my eyes. What young guy wouldn't jump at the opportunity for free booze?

"You can't imagine." He shakes his head. "But that's the kind of guy I am. I'll jump right in there and take the bull by the horns when no one else wants to." His tone is teasing, but he probably thinks he's all that.

And he is.

Tall and thick-chested with shoulder length blond hair, he can get any girl he wants and probably has had most of them.

He's captain of the hockey team at Boston University and, from what I've heard, an animal on the ice. And if I had to guess, I'd say between the sheets too.

They don't call him 'Wilde Man' for nothing.

I've heard too much about his love 'em and leave 'em ways from Sophie. I know she wanted me informed so I would keep my distance.

What she doesn't understand is being aware of his hook ups doesn't turn me off like you'd think it would. It makes me assume he must be really good between the sheets from all that practice.

Clancy is the worst kind of player there is because he's also a nice guy. And it would be all too easy to fall for him without meaning to.

He leaves a trail of broken hearts behind him wherever he goes. Even I'm susceptible to his handsome face and charming personality.

And let's not forget that hard body.

The bartender returns, placing my drink on a napkin in front of me. Eyeing the beverage skeptically, I can't help but wonder what it will taste like.

Golden in color, it looks harmless enough, but Clancy rattled off the liquor content, so I know it's going to pack a punch.

His Jameson gets set on the bar and he immediately raises the glass to his lips for a sip. "Come on. Don't make me drink alone." He tips his chin toward my drink. "Try it. I'm interested in hearing what you think."

Uncrossing my arms, I hesitantly close my fingers around the tumbler. It's cold against my skin.

"Go on. It's not going to bite you. At least not right away." He laughs.

It's his amusement at my expense that goads me into raising the glass to my lips and knocking it back in one continuous gulp. I don't stop until every drop is gone. Raising my head, my empty hand lands on my tingling lips.

I try not to cringe from the sweet aftertaste in my mouth, followed by a fiery burn down my esophagus and into my stomach. It feels like I swallowed a tiny fire breathing dragon.

The ice in the empty glass clinks together as I place the tumbler on the bar. A weary warmth envelops my limbs, instantly relaxing me.

Clancy watches for a reaction. "So? What did you think?"

Hmm. What do I think?

"It was better than I thought it would be. It's definitely sweet, almost too much so. And it feels a little like I swallowed fire." Licking my lips, I taste a bit of the lemon-lime mixed with the apple, or maybe I'm just imagining it. Either way, it's not as unpleasant as I expected.

"The second one will taste even better," he states.

"Second one? I don't think my stomach can take another. It might already be flaming."

"Trust me. I know what I'm talking about." He winks and gestures to the bartender for two more drinks.

"Okay, but this is the last one. I don't want to get drunk and feel like crap tomorrow morning. I plan on making the most of this weekend."

"You mentioned before that you can handle a lot, so I think you'll be fine."

He's so annoying for throwing my own words back at me. I'm going to have this one last drink and after that, if Clancy doesn't find somewhere else to be, I will.

I'm not going to let him weasel his way past my defenses, or into my panties, like so many girls do.

I'm smarter than they are.

But do I want to be?

Our drinks get pushed along the shiny bar top toward us. Clancy tucks two twenty dollar bills down into the tip cup and hands my glass to me. He picks up his own and holds it up in the air.

"I think a toast is in order."

"Why?"

"Because this is a happy occasion and it's the first time we've had a chance to talk in a long time." He leans closer.

"I'm not sure what you mean. We've never really talked much."

"Well, maybe we should rectify that." His voice lowers becoming impossibly deep.

I angle my torso toward him. "Okay. Whatever floats your boat, dude." My words contradict my body language.

"Don't sound so happy at the prospect. Look, I'll even make the toast, all you have to do is say cheers. You can handle that, right?" I shake my hand like I'm holding a pom pom and he grins. "To friendship... close friendship."

I mutter, "Cheers." And ignore his innuendo.

There.

My duty is done.

Now to finish this drink and get away from all this suffocating machismo before I collapse under the weight of it. I don't want to be one of those girls who give in easily. He should have to put in some effort for a change. I drink down this Devil's Advocate slightly slower than the first one, but when all is said and done, it's still pretty fast. I want to get away from Clancy ASAP.

No. I *need* to.

He's looking a little too attractive and he smells amazing.

I've been breathing shallowly for the past ten minutes trying to convince myself I was imagining it, but I'm not.

Trying to resist him after wanting him for so long is taking more restraint than I have. How do I ignore this opportunity when I may never get the chance to be with him again?

Setting the empty glass down, I lean toward him and sniff. He smells like sex in the woods. Okay, he looks like sex. But he smells like a combination of pine and wood, very manly.

"Did you just smell me?"

"No. My allergies have been bothering me and I was just making sure my nasal passages are clear."

What the fuck?

It's not the greatest answer, but hey, it's on the fly.

"And are they?"

"Yeah, you smell great."

Dammit.

He smiles triumphantly and grabs my hand. "Let's dance."

I'm trotting along beside him before I can disagree. "Wait. I don't want to dance with you." I put up a token resistance and try to tug my hand free, but I want to be in his arms. Judging from the sly grin twisting his lips, he knows it too.

"Well, I want to dance with you. Come on. How bad can it be? Just one dance."

Sighing, I give in and go with the flow, letting Clancy draw me into his arms. Agreeing is the path of least resistance. That's what I tell myself anyway.

Those two drinks have what little resolve is left waning and my body feels languid and loose enough to relax against him.

Of course, a slow song would have to be playing. Silently I cheer and curse the universe at the same time.

Molded to the front of Clancy's muscular body is the last place I should be.

But it might be the only place I want to be now that I am.

Which makes me a dumbass because I know he's a top-notch player and I'm not supposed to get played by him.

But is it getting played when you go into the situation with your eyes wide open?

Sophie, his own cousin, has warned me to stay away from him. Therefore, I'm not supposed to be dancing closely with Clancy, and I'm definitely not supposed to be enjoying it.

I probably shouldn't be so excited about the prospect of placing a check mark next to his name in my old diary. My stomach leaps and twirls. I shouldn't be, but I am.

Who knew that dancing could feel so sexual? That every particle that makes up my body could hum with awareness? That every brush of our hips teases me to the point I might splinter?

His large hands wander over my spine, sending chills plucking down each vertebra like fingertips on guitar strings.

His palms are hot against my lower back, caressing me. Making me want them to slide lower and cup my ass.

When his actions mimic my thoughts, my breath stutters. One cheek in each hand, he squeezes, urging me closer to his obvious hard-on.

Well, this escalated fast.

"You're driving me crazy," he confesses in a hoarse voice with his lips against my ear. "Holding you is the best thing about this wedding."

"I'm not going to fall for your bullshit," I inform him, leaning closer.

But who am I kidding?

I fell the moment I saw him standing next to me.

"Noted. But you don't have to fall for me to fuck me. So, what do you say?" He grinds into me and I let out a low moan, my eyelids sweeping shut. "You know it will be mind-blowing. Fuck. You're halfway to an orgasm already."

My eyes snap open with annoyance. Is it possible to want to screw someone and strangle them at the same time?

"So are you. How do I know you won't... " I struggle for a polite way to say what I need to. "End early."

He laughs. "I won't. And even if I did, it wouldn't keep me down for long." He winks. "I recover fast."

I curl my upper lip at him, but it's really at myself. I hate being so tempted by his hard, hot body. But I'm pretty sure he could tempt a nun to throw caution to the wind.

Besides, I haven't had sex in too fucking long.

In fact, I can't even remember how much time it's actually been.

But none of those reasons matter. What it boils down to is that I've never been the girl to doubt myself or to not go after the things I want.

I want Clancy Wilde.

He's been an object of my desire for years now. He's smoking hot and I'm pretty sure sex with him won't make me regretful.

You only live once, and tonight I'm going to grab onto Clancy and enjoy the ride.

CHAPTER TWO

Clancy

I REMEMBER THE FIRST TIME I MET TENLEY DURING ONE OF my summer visits to my aunt and uncle's house. She and Sophie walked into the kitchen when I was eating cereal at the table and I almost choked.

Stunned by her beauty, I quickly got my shit together and turned on the charm. Sophie narrowed her eyes and told me to forget about it or she'd cut my dick off. And out of respect for her, I did.

I have.

Until now.

God, Tenley's gorgeous. Over the years, her body has filled out, maturing in all the ways that have guys wanting to be near her, desperate to have her. I stare down at her and marvel that anyone can possibly be this attractive. With her wide, light eyes and pouty, red lips begging for my kiss, she's all I see.

When she's near, she overshadows every other woman present.

Tenley's the type of girl who could overshadow everything; even the goals I've set for my future. And that makes her a dangerous woman to be around.

No pussy is worth that. I should walk away now, while I still can.

"So, what do you say? Want to work out this attraction we share?" I ask, knowing there's no way in hell I'm leaving without getting her underneath me.

"What makes you think I want to have sex with you?"

"Don't you?" I arch a brow knowingly.

It's cute how she pretends she doesn't want me.

"We can't leave early and there's no way I'm walking out of here with you. I'm not advertising that we're about to screw." She avoids answering my question outright, but I still get the answer I'm hoping for.

"Gotcha. No one can know." I nod my agreement. That works for me. If this is going to be a one-time thing, I don't want anyone to think less of Tenley. We're both single adults and can do whatever we want. That doesn't mean anyone else needs to know. "Where do you want to rendezvous? I'm staying with Sophie at Miles' house while I'm in town. It might be awkward if we're together there. Especially since she dragged me here as her plus one since Miles couldn't come."

"What you really mean is Sophie would kick your ass all the way back to Boston. If she didn't cut your dick off first."

"Damn right she would. But I also need to stay on her good side. Jane is just one of our cousins. There are a lot more single ones where she came from. I see a lot of family weddings to attend in my future."

"You can come to my house. My parents are out of town and I have the place to myself."

"I hope you have a king sized bed just waiting to be utilized."

"I have a bed, and a comfortable one at that. It'll have to be good enough."

"You're right. Beggars can't be choosers. I'll take you naked wherever I can."

I rap on the door and my pulse jumps excitedly.

"I'm coming," she calls out, and I'm excited to know she didn't chicken out. I wondered if she'd follow through, or if the hour between the reception and now would be too much time for her to get lost in her own doubts.

I figured there was a fifty-fifty chance she might talk herself out of answering the door.

As I wait, I run through a mental checklist. And I can honestly say I've never done this before. I've never cared enough to be invested in what the other person thought. That's not the case with Tenley. If I'm only getting one time with her, I want to make it unfuckingforgettable.

Showered - check

Deodorant - check

Teeth Brushed - check

Non-holey boxer briefs - check

I rake my fingers through my hair before she opens the door.

She looks like a scared rabbit with her bright blue eyes as wide as they can be.

Smiling reassuringly, I take hold of her arm before she can nervously hop away. "Hey, there." I back her inside the room and release my hold as I close the door behind me. "Get naked," I order.

Her mouth opens in a perfect circle. "Wha... what?"

I bark out a laugh. "I'm joking. I just wanted to take your

mind off everything by making you laugh. I guess it didn't work out as I planned."

"Oh. Ha ha." She tosses a token laugh my way.

I catch hold of her hand. "Come on." Leading her into the room, I draw her into my arms. "I didn't get to dance with you nearly enough. And there were eyes watching us from all directions."

She places her hands on my shoulders. "You noticed that too, huh?"

We slowly sway from side to side, our bodies brushing teasingly against one another as I hum an unknown melody.

I nod. "It was hard to miss all their heads pinging in our direction. But now we're alone and no one else will know what happens behind these four walls."

"They better not," she scoffs.

"Do you really think I'd kiss and tell?"

"Oh come on. I know how guys are. And you jocks are the worst. You all love to boast about the pussy you get."

My dick twitches at her use of the word pussy. "Hey, I give you my word I wouldn't do that. But if it makes you feel better, we live seven states away from each other. What would be the point of bragging? No one would know who I was talking about."

"Yeah, but you can brag about a conquest without naming the person."

"You're more than a conquest to me, Tenley. You shouldn't compare yourself to anyone else."

"I bet." She rolls her eyes.

She's not going to believe whatever I say and there's no use wasting time that can be spent slicking my tongue between her long legs, pleasing both of us.

Damn. I can't wait.

Cupping her cheeks with my palms, I study her expression for a sign that she's not on board with what's about to go down.

My cock butts against the zipper on my pants like an angry bull ready to break free of the gate.

She licks her lips, never losing eye contact with me. It's sexy as fuck, and the last rope tethering me away from her unravels.

I crash my lips to hers, too hungry to be gentle. Hot and soft, her mouth yields under mine, parting for my tongue. Sweeping inside, I seek out and explore every part, swallowing down the sweet taste of her.

Tenley's nails dig into the tops of my shoulders urging me on, and my fingertips snake under her shirt hem, gripping her hips. Tugging her closer, I rock her softness against my hardness.

Fuck me.

This is going to be better than I imagined. We've barely begun and I can already tell.

Sparks fly between us, like a fucking fireworks show, as our tongues thrust and parry. She pushes on my chest and I draw back.

"Let's go upstairs," she suggests.

Grabbing her hand, I lead her to the staircase. Ushering her in front of me, I watch her ass jiggle through her sleep shorts as she jogs up each step.

Jesus.

She's temptation personified.

Forget the apple; Tenley is my original sin and I plan to devour her completely.

When we reach the top, my arms wrap around her waist and my face lowers until my nose is buried in the crook of her neck. Inhaling the fruity scent of her skin has me wondering what she'll taste like. Knowing I'm about to find out has my rigid cock painfully restrained in my pants. She has to feel it poking her ass. He's as eager as I am to get inside her any way he can.

We move down the hallway, her in front and me behind. Both of my hands glide over her tank top to cup her full breasts. Her taut nipples tease my palms and I know she's bare under the thin cotton.

My thumbs brush the rigid peaks and she moans, leaning her head back against my chest. My hips cradle her ass as my steps keep us progressing forward until we enter her bedroom.

The queen sized bed against the opposite wall seems too far away. Scooping Tenley into my arms, I stalk across the space and toss her onto the mattress. She bounces three times and peals of laughter escape her lips.

Pausing beside the mattress, I toe off my sneakers and tear my socks from my feet before I place a knee on the bed, joining her.

Lowering my torso, I run the tip of my nose up her neck, placing gentle kisses along the curve of her chin. My lips graze along her smooth skin until my teeth tug the bottom of her earlobe.

She gasps and bucks her lower body upward, showing me she's just as eager for what's about to go down as I am.

Kneeling, my fingers hook into each side of the waistband on her shorts and I slowly peel the material down her long legs, revealing her lack of panties and the neatly groomed snack I'm about to consume.

Fuck me.

My mouth waters at the sight. I have to touch her and see if she's as soft as I imagined. Reaching down, I trail my fingers along the slim strip of dark hair, over her clit, and along the edge of her lips. She's so pink and smooth like silk, I have to repeat the motion twice more.

She moans, raising her hips, hungry for more. I slip two

fingers inside her, pumping them as she rocks against my hand.

Holding my fingers up, I show her the visible proof of her eagerness. "You're so wet and hot. I can't wait to slide my cock inside you for the first time."

"What are you waiting for?" she moans.

"Uh-uh, not so fast. I need you completely naked. I want to see every single inch of you as I take you."

She raises her back, tearing her tank top over her head. "There. Naked." She falls back on her pillow and stares up at me, a challenge in her eyes.

Gripping the neck of my t-shirt, I tug it over my head and drop it to the floor. Her eyes hungrily roam over my bare torso, honing in on my stomach.

She licks her lips. "That looks like a lot of time spent in the gym."

"Oh it was, but the way you're looking at me makes it all worthwhile."

Her gaze climbs, studying my chest and shoulders. "You might have the perfect body."

I grin as I move backward, lowering to my stomach. "Now, enough talking. I'm starving and ready to eat." I delve my tongue between her lips and spear the end into her pussy, wiggling it around.

"Oh God," she gasps, her hands clutching my head.

"You taste so fucking good."

Sliding through her slit, I pluck her clit between my lips, gently sucking. She mindlessly rocks against my mouth as my tongue whisks over her swollen bundle of nerves. "Come on, let go."

Eyes closed and head tipped back, the graceful column of her neck tempts me. I want to bite the delicate flesh, but it can't compete with the satisfaction of devouring her pussy.

Flicking and circling the swollen flesh repeatedly, I drive

her toward release.

"I need you to flood my mouth with your juices," I growl against her clit.

Her fingers tangle in my hair as she grinds against my face. An encouraging rumble climbs from my chest and slips from my lips. I want her to rub her pussy all over me.

Painfully hard, I need some relief soon. My hips move, rubbing my dick against the mattress. Burying myself inside her sweet little cunt will be worth all the discomfort I'm dealing with now.

My fingers glide back inside her, hooking and stroking as my mouth continues to suck on her slick flesh.

Her legs twitch and she releases a long 'oh' as she comes.

I lap up all traces of her orgasm and wipe my mouth on my forearm.

Rising to my knees, I grab a square packet from my pocket and undo my shorts, pushing them and my boxer briefs down my thighs. Quickly maneuvering free of them, I manage to get the condom on in a matter of seconds.

I lower until I'm hovering over her, our lips only inches apart.

"Tenley. I'm going to make this a night you never forget."

Wrapping her leg around my hip, she throws her weight into the motion, driving me to my back and straddling my hips.

"I'm going to make this a night *you* never forget," she tosses my words back at me, gripping my cock and guiding it to her entrance. She sinks slowly down with a moan until I'm fully sheathed inside her.

"Christ." I grit my teeth. Wet, tight, and hot, her pussy envelops my dick even better than I imagined. She's got the creme de la creme of cunts, and tonight, every inch of her is mine.

Rolling her hips, she rides me slowly; prolonging the

torturous pleasure. My hands cup her tits, palming her nipples as I squeeze their fullness.

Watching her slide up and down my length, I get lost in the sensation until my eyes are practically rolling into my head.

I turn, flipping her under me and drive my cock into her harder and faster. My patience is gone. Now it's all about fucking her and owning her pussy.

We may only have tonight, but I'm going to make damn sure she remembers me forever. I already know that I'll never forget this interlude, and neither will my dick.

"Yes," she moans. "Harder."

Harder? Fuck yeah.

Forget soulmates.

This girl might be my sexmate.

Gripping her shoulders, I pull her back with every thrust forward I make. She grips my wrists, digging her nails into my skin as our flesh slaps together.

"Don't stop... close." Her heels in my lower back urge me on and her words have me seeing red with lust. No matter how incredible this is, there's no fucking way I'm finishing before she does.

Staring down at her full tits jiggling makes it more difficult to clamp down on my control. Sweat beads on my brow as I continue driving my cock into her.

Tenley arches, tipping her head back as she comes with a gasp on her pouty lips.

The first contraction of her pussy on my cock is all it takes for me to let go. Releasing all restraint, I crash into my orgasm full throttle.

"Fuck," I shout, completely overcome with the power of this release as I thrust inside her for the last time.

I've never felt anything like this. My vision blurs and I fall down on top of her.

CHAPTER THREE

Tenley

His hair tickles my chest as he lies there. My fingertips caress up and down his spine.

I can't believe I just had sex with Clancy Wilde.

I'm sure I'll freak out about this tomorrow, but right now, I don't feel anything but pleasantly sated. My entire body is limp like a cooked noodle and I swear his cock is still hard inside me.

Is that even possible?

He raises his head with a groan and smiles down at me.

Damn, he's gorgeous.

"That was amazing," he states, sliding free from my pussy.

Grabbing some tissues from my nightstand, he takes care of the condom. Backing up, he slips from the bed, heading into my adjoining bathroom. He returns seconds later with a warm, wet washcloth and proceeds to wipe between my legs.

I've never had a guy do this for me before. It was definitely unexpected coming from Clancy. I don't know why, but I pictured him immediately rolling over and falling asleep. Or thanking me and throwing his clothes back on.

I couldn't have been more wrong.

After he drops the cloth in the dirty laundry basket, he settles beside me on the bed and pulls me onto his muscular chest.

"You're awfully quiet. Is everything okay, or are you regretting this already?"

"What's to regret? It was fantastic," I reply.

"You're right, it was. But I also know that regret is bound to set in for you. Me, however, I'll never regret what just transpired. That was the best sex I've ever had."

"Really?" I sound more skeptical than I'd like.

"Really. I can't wait to do it again."

"Who said anything about doing it again? I was planning on going to sleep soon."

"Sorry, but there's not going to be a whole lot of sleeping tonight. You can't expect me to waste this opportunity to bury myself in your superior pussy again."

"Well, when you say it that way, it's more appealing."

"It's the truth. There will be a lot more orgasms, and I was about to add at my hand, but that's not really accurate. I plan on using my mouth and dick too."

God, I love his dirty talk. Not every guy can pull it off, but he can. Maybe it's because he has the skills to back up the words and that's why it works so well. He owns it.

Whatever the reason is, I hope he doesn't stop.

"Are you going to tell your cousin we had sex?" I ask.

"No, of course not. She'd cut my balls off with a dull, rusty knife."

I giggle at the visual.

"What? You think that's funny?" he questions in mock outrage.

"A little."

He cups his junk. "Not for me. I think the Wilde man just retreated. I might have an innie now."

"The Wilde man?" I snort and roll my eyes. "You're not too arrogant."

He moves his hand, revealing how well endowed he is, regardless of his joke.

"Hey, there's a difference between being arrogant and being confident. Don't confuse the two."

He has reason to be confident, even arrogant, if he can deliver like he just did every time.

"How long are you in town for?" I place my chin on his chest and stare up at him.

"I'm only here until tomorrow night. I have to get back for hockey practices. Why? Are you going to miss me?" He grins.

"Yeah, that's it." I barely restrain my eyes from rolling. But in a way, I will. And I'll definitely miss his body.

"I figured as much," he continues.

"Do you live on campus, or are you in an apartment?" The question seems random, but I want to know more about him. This is the first time I've had an opportunity to talk to him like this.

And it's awkward as fuck that it's after we've already screwed.

But better late than never.

"I'm actually the president of the fraternity I belong to and I live at the frat house."

"Oh geez."

"What's that supposed to mean?"

"I can imagine what life at the frat house is like; non-stop parties and half naked girls throwing themselves at you twenty-four-seven."

"I'm not going to say it's not crazy at times, but mostly it's just a bunch of guys hanging out together."

"Sure. Tell me another story."

"I'm serious." He tenderly sweeps a strand of hair from

my face. "You have a different image of who I am in your mind than how I actually am. I'm pretty tame. I workout a lot and train hard. I don't do relationships, but that doesn't mean I fuck every girl who looks my way. I'm actually pretty selective. You should be honored I chose you." He chuckles, infuriating me more than his words already have.

"Are you joking? Because if you're not, I swear to God I'm going to junk punch you when you least expect it."

He laughs louder. "You're such a little hellion. Is it weird that your threat turned me on?"

Narrowing my eyes, I glare unblinkingly at him.

"I'm just fucking with you. I don't expect you to be honored, unless you want to be. But I was serious about being selective. I've had my eye on you forever."

"You have?" I blurt out the question.

"Why does that surprise you? You're gorgeous. What sane man wouldn't want a shot with you?" His hands trace my skin lighting my nerve endings on fire.

I shrug. I don't want to tell him there have been plenty who haven't.

"You're the kind of girl a guy loses his mind over."

"But not you," I state.

"No, not me. Not because I don't think you're worth it, but because hockey is my main focus. And that's the way it has to be. She's the only girlfriend I can have in my life. She's demanding, time consuming, and comes before all others." As he talks his hands never leave my body, caressing my skin as if he can't get enough of the way it feels.

"I get it. Sophie has always been so focused on school. I know it's comparing apples and oranges, but the drive is there in both situations. Maybe it's in your gene pool. I tried to lure her out to more parties than I can count when we were in high school and she never gave in. Her focus was laser sharp and it's paid off for her. She's about to start her second year of college at King University."

"You go to King too. You're obviously a good student," he points out.

"I am, but I'm not top of the class like Sophie will be. I do well, but a mediocre test score isn't going to send me into a tailspin."

"What are you majoring in?"

"Education."

"You want to be a teacher?"

"Yep. I'd like to teach middle school age, so I can make a difference in their lives. I think that's an impressionable age, and a great teacher can help them enjoy attending school."

"You're right. I work with troubled youth. My mom has a pottery shop and we have a painting class for at-risk youth twice a week. A lot of the kids who we see are products of their environment. They want more for themselves, but don't know how to go about getting it."

"That's pretty cool that you help them out in that way. I bet they enjoy having a creative outlet."

"They do. It's also a great opportunity for them to relax. They know they're safe while they're at Mom's shop."

"Between school, hockey, and helping out the troubled youth of America, you must not have much free time."

"I don't. Which is another reason why I don't have a girl-friend. I've never met a girl who would be happy with the limited amount of time I can offer."

"Yeah, I understand. I've never been one to want to merge my life completely with someone else. I've had boyfriends, and I think they're always surprised and maybe even disappointed at how unclingy I am. I think I make them insecure because I don't act like I need them."

"Guys do like to feel needed," he offers. "I'm guilty of that myself."

"Yep, and I don't like needing someone, so that doesn't work in my favor."

"Not every guy wants a girl who hangs on his every word."

"How do you know? You said yourself that you don't want a relationship."

"I don't. But if I did, I would want a partner I could consider an equal and not a yes girl. Brains are as much of a turn on as beauty. Maybe even more so."

I laugh.

"What?"

"I'm sure you've thought, 'God her brain is so hot. I have to fuck her.'"

"It could happen." He grins.

"Sure. Keep telling yourself that."

"So, you never mentioned where you live."

"I have an apartment with a couple of friends. We've been living there for a year now. It's on the edge of King's campus."

"You weren't in the dorms last year?"

"Nope. I couldn't wait to be out of them. Although, with Sophie being a sophomore, I'll still be spending plenty of time visiting her there. Last year she didn't have a roommate, so it worked out great. What are the chances of her getting that lucky two years in a row?"

"What do you think of Miles?"

"He's a great guy. I've only heard good things about him."

"Good. He seems it to me too. I've only met him a few times, though. I'm assuming being her best friend, you'd know better. Sophie must tell you all the details of their relationship."

"There's nothing for you to worry about. You don't have to play the protective cousin."

"I'm not playing anything. That's just who I am."

I've seen his protective side in action on more than one occasion and I find it immensely attractive. What girl doesn't like a stand-up kind of guy? Someone to defend her honor and keep the assholes at bay.

"Do you still have a crush on Sophie's oldest brother Luca?" he asks, catching me off guard.

"What?" I play dumb.

"Come on. I'm not blind. Anyone who sees the two of you together can tell. You're not very good at hiding it." He grimaces.

Does it bother him?

My mouth opens and closes as I struggle to answer, but then I decide to be completely honest with him. Clancy and I are just having one night of sex, not a lifetime commitment. Even if his touch seems like more and so does the way he watches me so attentively.

"I've always thought he was hot. I still do. If he paid me any attention, I'd probably jump at the opportunity to spend time with him and see what he's really like." Although, after the hot sex we just had, I want to say 'Luca who?'

He nods, studying my face. I can't tell what he's thinking and curiosity gets the best of me.

"What? Don't hold back now."

"You're a smart girl. Do you really think you have a chance with someone like Luca?"

"What's that supposed to mean?"

"He's a lot older than you."

"Miles is thirteen years older than Sophie."

"He's not Miles and you're not Sophie."

"Yeah, I know. I'm not perfect like Sophie is." I love my best friend and I'm not trying to slight her at all. I'm just annoyed he's offering his opinion on this subject at all. Even if I may have asked for it.

"I didn't say that. And that's where you're wrong. Any guy would be blessed to have you as his girl. Hell, if I didn't have plans for my future, I would ask you out."

"You would?"

"Damn right, I would."

A smile teases the corner of my lips. I'm not sure why his reply pleases me so much. I guess it's because Clancy is someone I've crushed on for years.

"Come here." He pulls me higher on his chest and holds me closer. "Let's grab a little shut eye and then I'm going to wake you up for round two."

My palm rubs over the warm skin of his chest as my eyes drift shut. I don't know if I've ever been this comfortable before.

Who would guess Clancy Wilde is a cuddler?

CHAPTER FOUR

Clancy

SLIPPING FROM THE BED, I STRETCH MY ARMS OVER MY head, cracking my back in two places. I snap, crackle, and pop like the cereal; one of the products of playing hockey since I was four years old.

Staring down at Tenley's naked form, covered only by a thin sheet, I fight the urge to crawl back in the bed and take her one more time.

But that would be a huge mistake.

After repeatedly exploring every inch of her throughout the night, I already know I'll never get enough of being with her.

The best thing for me to do is to slip out while she's still sleeping to avoid any awkwardness and temptation.

Plucking my clothes and shoes from the floor, I cast a final glance her way as I leave the room.

Standing in the hallway, I tug on my clothes and slip my sneakers on my feet. Rubbing my hands up and down my face, I scrub the sleep away. Raking my hair back, I comb my fingers through the long strands and glance at my watch. It's only eight a.m.

I imagined sleeping in with Tenley and waking with her in my arms. But that was before I realized how addictive she is.

And it's not just her body, although that's freaking fantastic. It's her personality too. She's also smart and funny. And not afraid to call me out on my bullshit, which doesn't happen very often where girls are concerned.

Actually, aside from Tenley, I don't think anyone ever has. They're all too busy trying to get with the captain of the hockey team. It's about my status more than being with *me*.

Jogging down the stairs, I head toward the front door and slip outside before I can change my mind. I check to make sure the door locked behind me and head for my truck.

The morning air lacks the mugginess that will be present later on. I breathe in the fresh Virginia air. I swear this state smells better than other states do. There's a freshness with underlying notes of flowers. I notice it every time I visit during the warmer months.

If I wasn't a Bostonian at heart, I'd consider moving down here. There are some great colleges in this area, but playing for the Terriers has been my dream since I was a pre-teen.

And living that dream is even better than I imagined.

When I get to Miles' house, I let myself in as quietly as possible and slip my sneakers off. Walking as silently as I can on my sock covered feet, I head toward the kitchen. I need some coffee if I'm going to fully wake.

"Well, well, well. Look what the morning dredged up." Sophie arches a challenging eyebrow at me over the cup of coffee in her hand.

"Good morning."

"If you're chipper this early on a Sunday morning then you must've gotten laid."

I laugh. "I never kiss and tell."

"Yep." She nods with her lips pursed distastefully.

"Think what you want. I can neither confirm, nor deny your statement."

"Good morning," Miles calls, entering the kitchen. He aims a smile at Sophie before meeting my eyes.

"Hey, how's it going?"

"It's going. I've got no complaints. Joey is still asleep," he mentions his almost four-year-old son.

"Thanks again for letting me crash here. I really appreciate it."

He waves his hand. "No problem. You made your cousin happy by staying with us."

Sophie nods. "You did. It's been great seeing you. What time are you heading back to Boston? Or can I convince you to stay for a few more days?"

I'd love to spend more time with her and get to know Miles better. Maybe I'd even be able to sneak off and be with Tenley again.

No. I reprimand myself.

Stop thinking that way.

That was a one and done only. There is no being with her again. Many a career has been ruined by guys thinking with their dicks instead of their brains.

"I'll hit the road by noon, so I can be home by seven or eight."

"I hope you don't hit traffic, but traveling on a Sunday night it's almost unavoidable."

"Yeah, it is what it is. Seeing my favorite cousin is worth dealing with traffic, though."

She playfully shoves my arm. "You're such a sap."

"Hey, Clance. How was your weekend away?" Oliver calls out

as he walks across the locker room. He sits down on the other end of the bench from me.

"It was great, but too quick. I wish I could've taken more time."

"How's your cousin doing?"

"She's good, thanks. She's in love with some older, single father. He's a cool dude, but I'm worried it won't end well for her."

"What makes you say that?"

"He's so much older than she is. How can there not be a world of difference in the way they think?"

"I don't think overcoming age gaps is that big of a deal. As long as you're similar types of people."

"I guess. I really hope you're right. I want to see her continue to be as happy as she is. Speaking of happy, what's going on with you and Stacey?"

"We're great, thanks. I'm a lucky man. Stacey is a dream girlfriend."

"Yeah, yeah. So you say. But you're still in college. We'll see what happens when you're out in the real world with adult worries."

"Nothing will change."

"Probably not. But you never know."

"Okay Mr. Skeptical, good luck finding a girlfriend with that attitude."

"I never said I wanted one."

Tenley's beautiful face comes to my mind. She's the only girl I'd even entertain the possibility of dating, and she lives seven states from me.

I don't know when I'm going to see her again. And when I do make it back to Virginia, she might not be happy to see me after the way I snuck out on her.

It was for the best, though. But try telling that to a girl who thinks they've been wronged and it's like banging your head against the wall. They're never going to admit you're right.

Leaning over, I lace up my skates in record time. I've been tying them since I was four years old. I can do it in my sleep at this point.

Rising from the bench, I grab my gloves and head across the locker room. Oliver is on my heels as we head down the hallway and out into the arena. Most of the guys are already on the ice when we step out there.

Coach Cutter claps his hands to gain the attention of all my teammates and waves, ushering them his way. "Okay, listen up. Since this is the first practice of pre-season, we're going to focus on drills and getting the rust off your blades, so to speak."

"My blades aren't rusty. I take care of them," Oliver calls out, grinning.

"Ha ha, smartass. It's a figure of speech and you know it. We have a new member of this team. He was highly sought after and we worked hard on recruiting him." He holds his hand out, gesturing toward Donovan Archer. He's the little brother of one of my closest friends, Nolan, who plays for the Terriers' football team. He also lives at the frat house with me, and now Donovan has officially moved in too. "If you haven't already introduced yourself, make sure you do. We want him to feel welcome."

The guys all call out a greeting to Donovan, but most of them live in the frat house, so they've already hung out with him.

"We're doing acceleration drills. Get in three groups on the blue line," he orders.

We all move to do as he says and I end up in the front of the middle group. I already know what he's going to have us do before he tells us. These drills are pretty simple, but coach loves to work on the basics.

"When I blow the whistle, you'll skate to the red line, stop, and skate back to this line and stop. Then you'll repeat it skating to the far blue line, stop, and skate back to this blue line. Once you're done, go to the back of the group and wait for your next turn. I'll blow the whistle before you begin."

There are a couple of groans from some of the upperclassmen. Working on basics sucks, but it's necessary.

"Save your complaints for someone who cares," coach barks, putting an end to the nonsense.

I glance at Oliver next to me and smirk. Once that whistle sounds, all bets will be off. I'm going fast and hard like always. I like to be the best at everything I do, even if it's something as simple as acceleration drills.

I practice on the ice three times a week during the off season. I have a coach I pay big money to and he works privately with me. We do endless drills and exercises to improve my skating and puck handling.

Continuing to make progress is important to me. I'm only twenty-two years old, and if I want to go pro, I can't work hard enough to make sure I succeed. Regrets are not something I want to live with. I'm going to do everything I can to make the NHL, and if I don't, at least I'll know I gave my all.

"Get ready," coach orders, gripping his whistle.

I bend my knees. Staying low is important. The shrill sound cuts through the arena's silence and I push off the inside of my back blade.

Keeping my weight forward, I alternate from the inside of one blade to the other, accelerating quickly. I stop at the red line, but it's also a start at the same time, so I use the momentum to spring into motion again.

I race back to the blue line and stop-start again, racing to the far blue line.

I'm aware of Oliver in my periphery on the right side and

Donovan on the left. They're both slightly behind me, but I pay them no mind.

Once I hit the blue line, I stop, snow flying from my blades as I propel myself into motion again. I fly back and cross the line a solid two seconds before Oliver or Donovan.

Pumping my fist, I head to the back of the group.

"Damn, I thought I had you," Oliver glides over, stopping next to me in his line.

I shake my head. "Dude, you're dreaming. You weren't even close."

"I'll get you next time," he states with conviction.

I laugh. "Keep telling yourself that."

We practice for another hour and I continue to beat out Oliver.

"Goddamn, how do you get me every time?"

I raise my shoulders in a careless shrug. "I've got skills, man."

"Yeah, that's it." Oliver smirks. "It's only day one. I'll get my revenge soon enough," he states optimistically.

Coach blows his whistle, cutting off my chance for a reply. "I'll see you guys on Wednesday. Don't be late. Just a heads-up-- we'll be doing more drills."

A chorus of groans resounds and I chuckle. I can do whatever coach needs all day long because I train year round. Some of my teammates hadn't put their skates on since the end of last season. They're going to be hurting by tomorrow.

Good thing we don't have practice until the next day. Although, sometimes the second day is even worse than the first when your muscles need recovery time.

We head into the locker room and I pull my gloves off. I catch up with Donovan and ask, "How's it going, man?"

He ticks his head in a quick nod. "So far, so good. That practice was a lot milder than I was expecting."

"Don't let how today went fool you. Coach will turn it up

a notch for the next one and by next week, most of the players will be limping home after practice."

"Good. I like a challenge."

That's one positive about Donovan that I've already noticed. He's a hard worker. As the captain, I'll take hard work over talent any time. Although in Donovan's case, I don't need to choose.

Sometimes the most talented skaters feel the most entitled, and since skating is so easy for them, they don't know the meaning of busting their asses on the ice.

"Let's go back to the house and grill some burgers and dogs. I'm starving," I suggest, taking a seat on the bench.

Oliver sinks down next to me. "Is that offer open to non-frat residents too?"

"What's the matter? Isn't Stacey making you dinner?"

"Nah, she's working late again."

"Uh oh, brother. Is working late code for spending time with another guy?"

"Hell no. She wouldn't do that to me."

I grin, leaning forward to unlace my skates. "I'm just fucking with you. And you know you're always welcome at the house, as long as you bring some beer with you."

CHAPTER FIVE

Tenley

"You and my cousin looked pretty cozy the other night," Sophie offers nonchalantly. But I know if she's mentioning it, she's concerned.

I've been waiting for her to bring this up for the past thirty minutes. We've been sitting on the couch in my apartment, painting our nails and talking about the wedding.

Clancy has been the massive elephant in the room. And now that she brought him up, he looms over me like a specter.

"We were just dancing." I shrug. I can pretend to be nonchalant too.

Sophie glances at me side-eye. "It looked more like sex with your clothes on."

I laugh. I can't help it. This situation is beyond bizarre. I had sex with one of my longtime crushes, and I can't tell my closest friend because it's her cousin.

Not to mention, it was the sex of my life before he snuck out the next morning.

It sounds like something from a cheesy talk show and not my actual life.

Especially the sneaking out part.

I'm still angry Clancy did that to me. I wasn't going to throw myself at him and beg him not to leave.

I went into the situation with my eyes wide open... my legs too. By leaving that way, he showed what a jerk he really is under his nice guy persona.

I don't regret sleeping with him. How can I when it was the single most amazing sexual experience I've ever had? But as far as things go now, he's dead to me.

"Come on. Lighten up. That's the way people our age dance. I can't help it if you're with an old man."

"Hey, Miles is thirty-four, hardly ancient. And he's a great dancer."

"Don't get all defensive. I merely pointed out what Clancy and I were doing was hardly unusual. And can you fault me for taking advantage of the situation? He's hot as burning coals. I figured one dance wouldn't hurt."

"Well, it's good it was only one dance because he didn't come home that night. I don't know who he went home with, but I'm glad it wasn't you."

"No, he didn't come home with me."

Technically I'm not lying. He came over after I was already home.

My insides twist into guilty knots. I've never lied to Sophie before, and never planned to. Omitting facts seems as bad as outright lying when it comes to my best friend.

Ugh, I can't think about it. Time to change the subject.

"I never got a chance to ask why Clancy went to the wedding with you instead of Miles."

"Our babysitter fell through, so Miles had to stay home with Joey."

"God, it's weird to hear you say our babysitter."

"Why?"

"Because you're twenty-one and in college. And here you are playing mother to a four year old."

"I'm not playing anything. I love Joey like he's my own son." Her eyes flash fire at me like the protective mother she's become.

I hold up my hands. "Whoa. I'm sorry. I didn't mean to offend you. I shouldn't have been so flippant. I know how much he means to you."

"Well, you did. I know Miles and I have only been together for a year, but he and Joey are the most important people in my life. There isn't anything I wouldn't do for either one of them."

"I can see that. And you know I'm happy for you."

"I do." She nods somberly. "I don't expect you or anyone else our age to understand my relationship with Miles. I know he's older, but that doesn't matter to me. When you meet the right person, it's not always how you imagined." She gestures toward me. "You'll see. When you meet Mr. Right, I'll be sure to remind you of this conversation. You can plan and plan some more, but I'm the perfect example of how love will find you when it's meant to be."

"I don't want you to defend your relationship. I love that you have Miles and Joey."

"I know you do. Maybe I'm being overly sensitive about everything. I've been really emotional lately and I don't know why."

"Oh jeez."

"Oh jeez what? Am I missing something?"

"You're not pregnant are you?"

Sophie laughs. "No way. I take my pill religiously."

I roll my eyes. "I'm sure you do." Sophie is so organized she has an alarm set to remind her. I've slept over at her dorm too many times not to remember.

"I'm not ready for school to start," Sophie whines, leaning her head back onto the top of the couch.

"Why not? You love school."

"I do, but it's such a time suck. And I want to spend more time with Miles and Joey, like I get to in the summer."

"The school year will pass by so fast, and you guys will make do with whatever moments you get."

God, it's times like this when I'm thankful for being single. I don't have to please anyone else or squeeze them into my schedule. There's no one to disappoint when I can't spend enough time with them. It's just me, myself, and I. And that's enough.

"I thought this was supposed to be a small get together?" I glance at my roommate, Cassie, with a *what the fuck* expression. "Is there anyone who attends King University who isn't here tonight?"

"Yeah, Sophie," Cassie replies.

I giggle. "You're right. She might be the only one, though. And she might be the smartest of us all. She's probably getting lucky with her hot boyfriend as we speak and we're jammed into this space with everyone else."

"Let's go out onto the back deck. At least the air will be fresh," Cassie suggests.

"Sounds good to me." I move toward the back of the house without hesitating and grab a beer from a cooler as we pass by.

"Hey, I'm going to hit the bathroom now," Cassie points to the door with a line eight deep.

I grimace and give her a thumbs up, continuing on toward the door. Once I step out onto the deck, the tightness in my chest eases. I can move around without bumping into anyone.

"Tenley, over here," Reid, King University's quarterback, calls out and I wander over. He points to the vacant seat near his. When I sit, I know what's coming. He's got a thing for my best friend. Or he did last year, but she was already with Miles at that point. Timing really is everything.

"How are you doing?"

"No complaints. What about you?"

He shakes his head. "It's all good. We started practicing a few weeks ago. That's been keeping me busy. How's Sophie doing?"

There it is. I knew it was coming.

"She's great, been busy with her boyfriend and his son."

I'm not going to pull any punches. He needs to realize nothing will ever happen between him and Sophie.

"I'm happy for her."

"You are?" I quirk a brow.

He shrugs sheepishly. "Yes and no. I'm jealous as fuck because she's a great girl. But I do want her to be happy."

"You're a better person than me. How are practices going? Are we going to have a better record this season?"

"We're looking strong. I expect great things."

"Awesome. What about the hockey team? How are they doing?"

"My friends that play say they're going to kick ass."

"Do they ever play the Boston Terriers?"

"I'm not sure, why?"

"I know someone on the Terriers and he's cocky as fuck. I'd like to see him knocked down a peg or two."

"What did he do to piss you off?"

"That's a story for another day." And I hold up my beer, cracking the can open. "And for many more of these."

"You never really told me how the wedding was. Did you have a good time, or was it lame like weddings can be?"

I smile and glance over at Cassie as we walk down the sidewalk toward our apartment. "You're the only girl besides me who thinks weddings are lame."

"I've never gotten the appeal, but maybe someday if it's mine, I'll change my mind. Then again, eloping sounds good."

"I'm with you. Who needs all that fancy schmancy shit? I'm not the poofy dress type. Give me some jeans and a tank top and take me for better or worse."

Cassie snorts. "Exactly. And the jeans are a nice touch. It must be hell to wear a giant white dress for an entire day."

"Right? Why don't more people feel this way? Whenever I wear white I spill on myself. Which is why I never buy white shirts. I can't imagine the damage I could do to a whole dress."

"Back to the wedding. Did anything good happen? As much as they suck, I still wanted to be there for Jane. I was annoyed it fell on the same day as my grandmother's birthday party. But I love my nana, so..." She shrugs.

"I had a decent time. It was open bar and the drinks were good."

"That's it? No hot guy to dance with?"

"Well..."

"I knew it."

"I did dance with Sophie and Jane's cousin Clancy. He goes to Boston University."

"Do tell."

"He's the captain of the hockey team, tall, built, blond with shoulder length flowing locks." I shake my hair out exaggeratedly and we both giggle. It probably wouldn't strike us so funny if we hadn't each had a few beers at the party.

"He sounds hot. Did you guys only dance, or is there more you want to tell me, but aren't sure if you should?"

"God, it's kind of annoying and awesome how you know me so well."

"I know, isn't it? But that goes both ways. You always call me out too. So spill the details now."

"Yes, ma'am." I salute her. "Clancy came over when I was at the bar when I may have been feeling sorry for myself."

"Uh oh. Pity party for one turned into two is never a good thing."

"Yeah, uh oh is right. He took advantage of the pity party moment and turned on the charm. He ordered me drinks and mentioned how he'd been interested in me for a while, yada yada."

"Wait." She holds up her index finger. "Don't yada yada me. No skipping over the good parts. I want all the juicy, dirty deets."

"It's not a big deal. He doesn't do relationships, but if he did, I might be the lucky one."

"He said that? Because that's a douchey thing to say."

"No, not really, but that's how I interpreted his words."

"Jeez, it's like pulling teeth getting you to share the good stuff. Did you guys fuck or not?"

Rolling my lips together, I flick my gaze to Cassie. "We did."

"Oh my God. You did? How was it?" she shrieks, bouncing up and down the sidewalk like a pogo stick.

"It was amazing."

"Did you tell Sophie?"

"No," I yell. "No, she can't know. She's been warning me to stay away from Clancy since the first time he and I met. She'd be so angry if she knew."

"Oh Lord. Is this going to cause an issue between you guys?"

"It shouldn't. Yeah, I feel horrible keeping the secret from her, but there's no reason why she'd need to know."

"Yeah, you're right. We all have secrets we have to bear. This will be yours, and after a while you won't even think about it anymore."

"Right. That's what I was thinking too. Clancy was a onetime thing and we'll never be in that situation again. In another sex months I won't even remember it happened."

"You mean six?"

"Huh?"

"You said sex months. If thinking about him flusters you that much, it must've been good." She laughs.

"You have no idea." I run a hand over my hair, smoothing back the long strands. Forgetting about my night with Clancy will be a tall order. But a girl's gotta do what a girl's gotta do.

CHAPTER SIX

Clancy

TWO WEEKS LATER

STARING TOWARD THE FRONT OF THE CLASSROOM, MY FOCUS shifts from the professor and his lecture on medieval art to a memory of holding Tenley in my arms while we danced at the wedding. Her snark-filled banter was entertaining and only made her more attractive. I love a girl who's quick witted and can give back as good as she gets.

Smiling as I think about it, I wish I could see her again. If only she lived in Boston. If she did, we'd have been screwing like rabbits for the past two plus weeks. Fun times.

As enjoyable as I know that would be, I also realize it's for the best that we're not in the same state. Neither of us would get anything accomplished. We'd spend all our free time in bed.

"Dude what are you smiling at?" Flynn smirks.

"I'm not." I scowl to cover up the fact that I was smiling and didn't realize it.

"Who is she?"

Professor Morse dismisses us, saving me from answering

Flynn's question. I grab my backpack and shove my laptop down inside.

"Dude, answer me," he presses.

"I don't know what you're talking about."

"Who is she? Come on. You're supposed to tell me these things."

"Flynn, you're with me all the time. When have I been with a girl lately?"

"Dude, that wasn't some random smile. That was a lovesick smile. Or a blow job of your life kind of smile."

I laugh, shaking my head as I zip my backpack closed. "Where do you come up with this shit?"

"Come up with what? I'm being serious and you're acting like I'm not."

"You have an active imagination."

It's not that I don't share things with Flynn, but I'm not ready to tell him about Tenley. He won't understand she's different for me than other girls.

I can't be with her, but that doesn't mean I'm not going to keep thinking about her and wishing I could.

"Okay, if you say so. I'm not going to push you." Flynn rises, shoving his phone into the pocket on his shorts.

Standing, I sling my backpack over my shoulder and start down the aisle. Once we're in the hallway, I spot Owen and hold my hand up in a wave. He waits for us by the front door and we exit together.

"What do you know about Clancy getting the blowjob of his life?" Flynn starts in right away.

Owen looks confused before grinning. "Don't look at me. I didn't give him one."

I bark out a laugh. "Flynn, let it go."

"Fuck that. You need to come clean."

"I'm not going to make some shit up so you feel better. Now shut the fuck up about it or get lost."

Jesus. He's more gossipy than some of the girls I know.

Owen looks between Flynn and me with a brow quirked questioningly. "I don't know what's going on, but I do know I'm starving. Anyone want to grab a bite to eat?"

Glancing at my watch, I check the time. I've got two hours until my hockey practice and I'm done with my classes for the day. I was going to run home and take a nap, but I'm better off eating something. A nap will make me feel sluggish, while food will refuel me.

"I have to get to the gym. I told Darren I'd meet him there." Flynn mentions another of our friends who lives at the frat house. "In fact, I need to hustle or I'll be late. I'll catch up with you guys later." He points at me. "Don't think I'm forgetting."

I hold my middle finger up in his direction and turn to Owen. "Let's eat. I need some energy for practice later."

"We had ours earlier, which is why I'm starving."

"Eliza didn't pack you a sandwich?" I mention his girlfriend. The two of them have been together for almost one year.

He grins. "She did. I ate it before practice."

We decide to grab a pizza at the nearest restaurant. There's a light crowd due to the early hour and Ron, the owner, notices us right away. He smiles as we approach the counter.

"Hey, guys. How's everything?"

"Hey, no complaints. What about you? I didn't get a chance to stop by over the summer," I explain.

Even though I stayed in the frat house, I never found myself in this area. I worked construction a few days a week and helped my mom out at her pottery shop the other two weekdays. I also trained in the gym and on the ice.

My schedule was pretty packed. I kept the weekends for catching up on everything I didn't get done during the week.

Not exactly the life most would expect from the president of the fraternity.

"Yeah, I noticed. Glad you're back. And what about you?" he directs the question toward Owen.

"I'm great, thanks. Sad that the summer is over, but glad that football season is about to start."

"You guys want your usual?" Ron's gaze bounces between us.

"I'm good with that."

Owen gives a quick nod. "Same."

We find an available booth and slide across the bench seats.

"Goddamn. I forgot how amazing it smells here." He draws an exaggerated breath in through his nose. "I'm so fucking hungry. Maybe we should've ordered more food."

I laugh because 'our usual' is enough food for six people.

"I feel like we haven't had a chance to catch up since I got back from Virginia. What's been going on with you?"

"I'm thinking of asking Eliza to marry me."

"Wow. I wasn't expecting that to be your reply. Congratulations, man. She's a great girl."

"Thanks. She's the best. I'm smart enough to know I want to spend the rest of my life with her. Anyway, I'm not doing it tomorrow. I've gone looking for a ring a couple of times, but I haven't purchased one yet. The only other person who knows besides you is Trevor. And I told my brother, Josh."

"Will you stay at the apartment you have?"

"Yeah, through the school year, and she'll stay in her dorm. After that, who knows where we'll end up. The rest depends on whether I get picked up in the draft or not."

I nod solemnly. This is our senior year and so much hinges on how our seasons go. I admire how he's able to juggle a girl-friend, school, and football, but our conversation reminds me of the importance of staying on task. I need to keep my focus on hockey.

Every day is a step closer to achieving my dream of playing in the NHL.

"Enough about me. I feel like I'm dominating this conversation. How was your trip to Virginia?" Owen questions.

"It was good. Pretty uneventful."

I'm not going to tell him I spent time with a girl who I really like. I'm not going to tell him I had the best sex of my life. Doing so would only validate my feelings for her.

It's time to erase Tenley from my mind once and for all.

Music blares from the large speakers in the living room. The bass thumping so forcefully it vibrates in my chest. Every piece of furniture has been rearranged, creating a wide, open space in the middle of the room.

Whenever we have a party, things have a way of getting out of hand. We've learned to expect the unexpected through trial and error.

Mostly error.

There are usually a couple of guys who'll start to wrestle and end up falling on the coffee table. Three coffee tables later, and I've finally smartened up.

"This never gets old," Flynn comments before tipping his beer bottle back for a deep pull.

Really? I don't know. I'm kind of over it already and it's only the first party of the year. We made it through the first week of school and normally that alone would be cause for celebration. I'm not sure why I'm so indifferent to it all when I never have been before. In fact, I'm annoyed by the noise and the number of people here.

Is this what maturing does to a person?

Good thing I'm graduating in the spring. By next fall I might've been calling the cops on my own frat party just to get rid of all these people.

Hell, it's early in the year, I still could.

"You don't agree?" Flynn questions.

"I don't know, man. I'm out of sorts tonight. All this noise is giving me a headache."

Darren, another of our frat members and close friends, saunters over with a new beer for Flynn and me.

I gesture to my still almost full bottle and silently decline.

Flynn reaches for his refill while draining the other at the same time.

Darren shrugs. "More for me." He sips from one bottle and then the other.

I shake my head, disgusted with his behavior and then shake it again, disgusted with myself for my disapproval.

What the hell's going on with me?

Maybe I need hard liquor tonight.

"Don't mind Clancy. He needs to get laid." Flynn smirks.

Is that it? Do I need to get laid?

"Clance has never had a problem with the ladies," Darren comments, having my back.

"No, I haven't. And I still don't." I wave at a group of girls staring my way. They giggle and smile flirtatiously, but I'm not the least tempted to pursue any of them.

A dark haired, blue eyed goddess dances through my thoughts, teasing me. If Tenley were here right now, I'd be spending the night buried inside her. Over and over I'd take her in the hopes of getting my fill. But I'm fairly certain it wouldn't do me any good. I'd still be in the same predicament when the sun rose.

Tenley is the drug I can't get enough of.

A commotion by the door catches my attention and I barrel my way through the crowd to find out what's going on.

"Hey," I shout, when I see the group of guys milling about the foyer. Brady, Nick, and Zeke, some of the former frat members who've since graduated, are back to honor the tradition of coming to the first party of the year.

"Big man," Zeke calls out, catching my hand for a quick shake and pulling me in for a hug.

"How's it going?" I ask.

"Great. Work's been busy, but I've got no complaints."

Nick is the next one to grab me in a bear hug. "Oh, I missed you," he fake sniffles in my ear.

"Get out of here." I laugh, shoving him away.

"How've you been?" Brady questions, slapping me on the chest.

"I've got no complaints. How about you? How's Harlow?"

"She's doing really well. Life is good."

"I'm glad to hear that." I smile, glancing between the three of them. "Thanks for coming and keeping the tradition alive."

"Are we the only ones?" Zeke seems surprised.

"So far, it's just you guys."

"Who needs anyone else when you've got us?" Nick is quick to reply.

"Exactly. Now maybe this party won't suck so much." I raise the bottle to my lips.

"I need one of those." Zeke points to my beer.

"The cooler's out on the back deck. You guys know the way."

The three of them move together like they still play on the same football team. Greetings are called out excitedly. These guys were extremely popular when they attended B.U. And not just with the ladies. They're the kind of athletes who inspired those around them to do better.

We step onto the back deck and I swear it groans in

protest. Between the four of us, that's a lot of weight in addition to all the other people already out here.

They grab beers and we settle at a table.

"Who's the new kid?" Brady asks, nodding his head toward Donovan.

"That's Donovan Archer, Nolan's little brother."

Brady smiles. "No kidding. Another set of brothers for this frat to survive," he jokes.

Trevor, one of my best friends and fellow frat members is Brady's younger brother.

"It barely survived the Lincoln brothers," I jest.

"Come on. We weren't that bad. Well, I wasn't. I can't speak for Trevor. I haven't been here for a couple of years. But now that Trevor's a married man, he's on a tighter leash."

"Ooh, taking a shot at baby bro and he's not here to defend himself. I like it." Nick, always the instigator, grins.

"It's not like that at all. I'm proud of him, and Grace is great for him."

"Who would've thought baby Lincoln would be married before you?" Zeke asks.

"Me. I did. Harlow and I are in no rush. She knows I'm all hers."

"I don't know how you guys all do it." I press my lips together and tick my head from side to side.

"Do what? Have girlfriends?" Nick questions.

"Yeah. I don't think I could make it work."

"I can only speak for myself, but when I met Carter, I fell hard. And I didn't have a choice in the matter. Being with her took precedence over everything else, football included. It didn't matter that I wasn't planning on being in a relationship. I got ready quick and pursued her like a motherfucker." He laughs.

"See, that's why I can't have a girlfriend. Hockey has to

come first. Girls are just a distraction I don't have the time or energy for."

"Who are you trying to convince, son?" Zeke asks, smirking.

"No one. I'm merely stating facts."

"You don't need to convince us. Do whatever works for you," Brady suggests.

"I hate to interrupt the life lessons, but I'm starving." Nick rubs his stomach.

"You, hungry? What a fucking surprise," Zeke drolls and we all laugh.

Glancing around the table, I take in the sight of my friends sitting here with me. I can't think of anywhere else I'd want to be right now. Life is good.

CHAPTER SEVEN

Tenley

"I LOVE COMING HERE FOR DINNER. IT SMELLS FANTASTIC. Thank you for having me, Miles." I raise the lid on the crockpot and drool over the meatballs.

"What about me? I'm the one who invited you," Sophie reminds.

"Miles is the one who cooks all the delicious food. I know who to thank."

"You're welcome anytime. Sophie really packs the food away, so I always cook extra," he teases.

"That's not entirely untrue," I point out.

"Joey is the biggest eater in this house now." Sophie runs a hand over his dark hair.

"I'm getting grown up," Joey announces, raising his head from the book he's flipping through at the kitchen table.

The doorbell ringing catches my attention. "I'll get that for you." I head to the front door and find Luca, one of Sophie's older brothers, on the other side. I've been crushing on him for as long as I can remember. He's always been the second name on my 'wish list'.

"Hey, Luca."

"Tenley, hi." He pulls me in for a hug and the usual spark of attraction isn't there. I pull back and frown. "Is something wrong?"

I compose my expression and smile. "No. I was wondering if I turned the coffee maker off before I left home and was retracing the steps in my mind."

God, I suck at lying.

"Did you?"

"Did I what?"

"Shut the coffee maker off?"

"Oh, yeah. I did."

I sound like a complete airhead.

"Good. I haven't seen you in months. How've you been?" He aims a smile at me. That same flash of teeth would normally have me weak-kneed and ready to do whatever he asked. Unfortunately, he's never asked me to do anything. And it's not like it wasn't obvious I would've been open to the idea of messing around with him.

I made it pretty clear.

Embarrassingly clear.

But now it's not even affecting me.

Am I coming down with something? I run my palm over my forehead. Nope. Still cool to the touch. What is going on? How did my crush on Luca Gardner dissipate?

Absence always makes my heart grow fonder when it comes to him. The only other person who has the same effect on me is Clancy.

Oh, shit. Am I not lusting after Luca because I've had sex with Clancy and it was so freaking amazing?

Ugh. I bet that's it.

Luca ducks down to study my face. "Are you sure you're okay? You seem a little out of it."

No. I'm not sure I'm okay at all. I don't want Clancy Wilde obliterating my other crushes.

Too late.

"Fuck."

"What's wrong?" He looks concerned.

"Oh, sorry. I didn't mean to say that out loud. I remembered I have a paper to finish for Monday."

His gaze remains on me, skating over my face and dipping down to the V of my neckline. When it returns, connecting with mine, he grins. "You look great, but you're acting weird."

Luca Gardner just checked out my tits. I witnessed it myself, and yet I'm not excited by the prospect of what it could mean.

Isn't this what I've always wanted? For him to see me as a grown woman and not his kid sister's best friend?

Too little, too late. Something bigger has come along. I picture Clancy's bare chest sliding over me and I smirk at the pun I've made.

"What are you thinking about?" He raises a brow.

He probably thinks I'm picturing him naked.

"This guy I met."

"Oh. That's not what I thought you were going to say."

"Yeah? Did you think I was picturing you naked or something?"

"Well, now that you mentioned it." He shrugs.

"Oh, Luca." I pat his cheek. "That ship has sailed. Come on. Your sister is going to wonder where you are." I lead the way into the kitchen.

"Hey, everyone."

"Luca." Sophie gives him a quick hug.

Miles wipes his hands on the dish towel before he shakes Luca's hand. "How's it going?"

"It's all good, thanks. What about you guys?"

Sophie hooks her arm through Miles'. "We're fabulous."

"I can see that." Luca notices Joey at the table. "Joey, buddy. How's it going?"

Joey's head snaps up at Luca's voice. "Uncle Luca," he shouts, sliding off his chair.

He holds out his arms and Joey jumps into them.

"Hey, big guy. What have you been up to?"

"I go to school, Uncle Luca."

Only an almost four year old gets that excited about attending school.

"You do? I bet you're the smartest kid there."

Normally, watching Luca with Joey has me ready to offer to birth his children, but today all I'm experiencing is the normal enjoyment at how cute they are together. This is so freaking weird.

Maybe I should send Clancy a thank you note. Thanks for the life-changing sex. You did the impossible. You cured me of my Luca crush once and for all.

Nah, screw that. It would only add to his impossibly large ego. And I'm being pathetic thinking about a guy I had a one-night stand with. I guarantee he's not losing any sleep thinking about me.

"Okay, guys. Grab a plate and dish up what you want. We're going to eat outside," Miles instructs.

"Is that your professor tone?" I joke.

His voice is deep and attractive. I picture Sophie sitting in his class last year, staring at him with hearts in her eyes.

"Huh?" Miles looks confused.

"Yep. That was it." Sophie wiggles her eyebrows.

I lean over, whispering in her ear, "It's kind of hot."

"Kind of?" She laughs, fanning herself. Their story is like something out of a porno. The babysitter falls for the single father and then goes off to college, only to find out he's her professor.

Once we're all situated around the table out on the patio, conversation trickles off as we eat the delicious meal.

The warm temperatures today are unusual, considering

the end of October is approaching. Fall is my favorite season, but it always passes so quickly. We slip into winter temps in November and don't warm up again for a few months.

"Dude, too bad your pool is closed. We could all go for a swim," Luca mentions.

"It's not that warm." I arch a brow at him.

"I've swum in colder water than this would be," he boasts.

"Was it on a dare?"

"Of course."

"What else have you done on a dare?"

"How much time do we have?"

"Enough for you to answer."

He glances at Joey. "I don't think this is the time to discuss my shenanigans."

Sophie snorts. "Is any time the right time?"

I open my closet door and stand on my toes to reach the pink box on the top shelf. My fingertips barely reach, but I manage to wiggle it forward until it tips from the edge of the wood. I catch both sides in my hands, setting it on the hardwood floor.

Sinking down, I sit and remove the cover, placing it to the side. Rifling through old birthday cards and letters, I continue to search for my old diary.

A glimmer of purple catches my eye and I dig through until I get to it. Jackpot. Here it is. Plucking it from the rest of the keepsakes, I open to a random page.

Today was a wonderful day. Sophie's cousin Clancy is visiting from Massachusetts. He's so hot!!!

My chin drops to my chest and I shake my head from side to side. Reading those words is embarrassing, but what's even worse than that, is how I could write the same thing now if he came to visit. Minus a few exclamation points. I still think he's hot and I get excited when he comes to visit.

Paging through the small book, I search for my 'wish list'. It takes me a few minutes because it's so short. Only two names. Clancy Wilde sits in the number one spot, followed by Luca Gardner at number two. And that's the extent of my list.

Jumping to my feet, I take the diary with me. Grabbing a pen from my nightstand, I sink down on the edge of my mattress, balancing the diary on my thigh. Tugging the cap off with my teeth, I draw a squiggly line through Luca's name. The black ink is stark against the white page and the purple ink I wrote with as a teenager. I trace over the wiggles, making it more pronounced.

It's strange how therapeutic this feels. I've had a crush on Luca for as long as I can remember. And at the advanced age of twenty-one, I'm finally ready to let it go. Removing him from my list is the final piece. The best part is, I'm not disappointed or remotely conflicted about it.

CLANCY WILDE.

I study the name written all in capital letters. My stomach flutters fast like a hummingbird's wings.

I underline his name and stare some more. Then underline it again. Why can't I cross it off?

I had sex with him, meeting my goal. The 'wish list' was all about sleeping with them.

My eyes trace over the shape of each letter like my fingertips and tongue did on each ripple of his abdominal muscles. A wave of heat assails me and I clench my legs together.

Pressing the tip of my pen to the page above his name, I ignore the fact that I'm a twenty-one year old woman and not a thirteen year old girl, and draw a large heart surrounding the eleven letters. Slamming the diary shut, I return it to the box in my closet and set it back on the shelf.

CHAPTER EIGHT

Tenley

"What's wrong with you? You're not looking so hot," Cassie offers, as I sprawl across the cafeteria table.

"I don't know. I feel like ass." My head is propped up on my palm and my eyes are slitted to avoid the harsh glare of the fluorescent lighting.

"That good, huh?"

"Pretty much. I'm achy and tired and I have a massive headache. It could be that I haven't been getting enough sleep and it's finally catching up with me."

"And it must suck that it's not even partying keeping you up."

"I know, right? I'm busting my ass studying. I'm not having any fun at all. Remind me why people enjoy the college years so much?"

"I can't believe Thanksgiving break is right around the corner. This year is flying by," Cassie offers.

"It really is. And I'm not ready for finals and they'll be here in a month. I used to think a month was so long when I was a kid, but now it feels like the equivalent of a couple of weeks."

"Are you going away for Thanksgiving?"

"Nah, my family does a big spread for dinner and my parents would probably disown me if I wasn't there for it."

"What are they going to do when you get a serious boyfriend or even get married? You might have to go to his family's house sometimes."

"I'll cross that bridge when I get to it. Right now, I have no boyfriend and no prospects lined up, so it's a non-issue."

My thoughts drift to Clancy and the night we shared. God that was an amazing time.

What's he up to these days?

He's probably having a lot of amazing nights with many different girls, and I can't really be salty about it. He was completely up front with me and I still slept with him.

It's not like I regret it, either. I just wish we'd had an opportunity to repeat the sex the next night, but he had to be back in Boston.

"Speaking of prospects, have you heard from Clancy at all?"

Is it obvious I'm thinking about him?

"No. I told you that was a one-time thing."

I'm not telling her how I've stalked his social media accounts for any glimpse of him. And he's just as gorgeous as I remembered.

"What about you? Where are you going for the holiday?" I ask, turning the conversation to Cassie. I can't deal with talking about Clancy right now. I might find myself admitting how he got under my skin and I can barely admit it to myself.

"Are you kidding? I've been looking forward to Thanksgiving dinner for months now. My mother is a fantastic cook. I'm going to stuff myself silly and make up for all the shit food we eat here."

"The food's not that bad." I raise a shoulder in a half shrug.

"It's not that good, either," she retorts.

"Right now, food is the last thing on my mind. I might need coffee given to me intravenously, though."

"Does this mean you're not going to come to the party tonight?"

"Oh shit. I forgot all about it."

"Is that a strong no?"

"It's a we'll play it by ear and see how I'm feeling."

"Isn't Sophie coming with us?"

"Yeah, she mentioned it."

"Why don't you head home and take a nap?"

"I've got one more class to make it through, and if I survive, I will."

We pause outside on the landing of the frat house stairs.

Sophie leans her head on my shoulder. "Thanks for hanging out tonight even though you're not feeling well."

"No problem. Just remember, if I die, my death will be on your conscience."

"I think you'll survive. Unless you drink hard liquor. Then you'll feel like dying for sure."

"I won't be drinking much of anything. My stomach is already queasy."

"Why don't you come back to Miles' house with me tonight? Then I can nurse you back to health. And Miles will cook for us in the morning."

"The idea of eating anything makes me want to vomit. Let me make it through this party and then I'll decide where I'm spending the night. Hopefully I won't be holding the porcelain god."

"Gross. I hope you're not contagious. I don't want to get sick."

"I'll try not to breathe." I snort and Sophie laughs.

We step inside the house and the noise level is ridiculous. Resisting the urge to plug my ears with my fingers, we move toward the kitchen. Cassie told us to meet her there, but with the number of people here, we'll be lucky if we spot her.

Checking the fridge, I grab a bottle of water for myself and one for Sophie. I know she's not going to drink since she drove us.

"Here." I hand over the bottle, cracking the cap on mine. Taking a small sip, my eyes scan the area for Cassie.

"It's hot as hell in here and it smells like a locker room. Maybe we should step out on the deck and get some fresh air," Sophie suggests, scrunching her nose.

"Sounds good." The air in the house is stale and thick with heat. It's stifling.

Sophie opens the back door and we exit the house. Immediately, I breathe a sigh of relief at the cooler temperature.

Cassie waves at us from a seat at the rectangular glass table. She's talking with Reid, but once he notices Sophie, his eyes light up. I shake my head. This dude needs a reality check. Maybe hearing Sophie talk about how happy she is with Miles will serve as one.

We slip into two empty chairs at the table.

"Hey, Sophie. How've you been?" Reid questions.

"Hi." She offers a small, tight smile. "I'm great, thanks. How about you?"

"No complaints."

"How are you feeling?" Cassie cuts in, glancing at me.

I shrug. "I'm not sure if I'm better or worse at this point. My head seems to hurt less, but I'm still exhausted. I'm not sure if I'm sick or if I'm just run down."

"You should sleep in tomorrow for as long as you can and see if you're better. If not, you can make a doctor's appointment. Maybe you have mono."

"Shit. I never thought of that. God, I hope not. I don't want to feel like this for another six weeks, or however long mono usually lasts."

"Don't worry about it now. Just get some sleep and see how you feel."

"Sophie, how are you and Miles doing?" Cassie questions with a smirk, and I know she's doing it on purpose. She's not trying to be cruel, but I suspect she has a thing for Reid.

"He's great. And you should see Joey. He's getting so big and talking up a storm." She beams proudly.

Reid's expression falls and Cassie places her hand on his arm, drawing his attention her way. I hope she knows what she's doing. Getting involved with someone who has feelings for another person is never a good idea. But she's an adult and can do what she thinks is best for her.

We hang out for a few hours and I enjoy myself more than I expected. I stop worrying about everyone and everything and relax. Clancy pops into my head, but I pushed him back out. I stick with water and by the time we leave, my stomach is feeling a little better. I'm convinced I'm just overtired and stressed out. If I can catch up on sleep, I'll be back to normal in no time.

Saturday mornings are usually my time to sleep in, but not this morning. I've thrown up so many times, my stomach muscles are sore. I'm weak and I don't know if I have the strength to go to the campus urgent care clinic.

Forcing myself to get dressed, I drag my feet all the way to my car. The clinic is only a few blocks away, and, due to the early hour, there are only a couple of cars in the lot. I'm able to park near the door, which is a good thing because I don't think I'm strong enough to make it any farther.

After I check in, I'm called to an exam room. The nurse checks my blood pressure and tells me to change into a gown. I don't bother because it's too much work. Instead, I lie down on the table and pray for death to take me.

The doctor knocks on the door before entering. "Hi, I'm Doctor Jones."

"Hi."

She glances at the laptop screen. "It says here you've been sick for a few days now. You're having fatigue, vomiting, and a headache."

"Yeah. I'm miserable."

"No fever at all?"

"No."

"When was your last period?"

I count backward, and try to remember when it was. "I'm not sure. I've never been on a regular cycle. Sometimes I skip them."

"If you had to estimate, when would you say it was?"

"Early August?"

Doctor Jones types on the keyboard. "Are you sexually active?"

"Yes, but not very often."

"When was the last time you were?" She holds her hands poised over the keyboard, waiting for my reply.

"The second week of August."

"Could you be pregnant?"

"No." I shake my head vehemently. "We were safe."

"Are you on birth control?"

"No. But we used a condom."

"Okay. I'd like to run a pregnancy test and rule out that possibility."

"I'm not pregnant. I can't be."

"Chances are this is just a horrible virus, but let's make sure." She opens a cabinet, removing a cup. "Here you go. Slip inside that bathroom and give me a urine sample." She points to the adjoining bathroom.

Sliding down from the table, I head inside the bathroom and do as she asked. When I exit the small room, I set the sample down on the counter and climb back up on the table. Running this test is a waste of time. I can't be pregnant.

There's no way.

"I'll be right back with your results." The doctor picks up the cup and exits the room.

I lie there alone for the next five minutes waiting for her to come back in.

I don't pull out my phone because I'm too tired to. At this point I just want answers, so I can feel better.

Doctor Jones steps back in with an unreadable expression on her face. "You're pregnant."

"Wait. What? How's that possible?"

"I'd guess the condom had a hole in it, but there's no way to know for sure. I can only deduce by what you told me."

Tears fill my eyes. Oh my God. I'm pregnant and I'm only twenty-one years old. What am I going to do?

"Are you and the father together?"

I shake my head as the tears flow down my cheeks.

Oh shit. I have to tell Clancy we're going to have a baby. We don't even live in the same state. How are we going to have a baby together?

And how am I going to break the news to Sophie?

She's going to be so angry with me.

"Do you know whether you'll have the baby or not?" Doctor Jones questions.

I nod. "I'm keeping it. I can't have an abortion. I won't be able to live with myself for the rest of my life if I did." Sweeping my fingertips under my eyes, I wipe the wetness away.

"Adoption is always an option for you. Let me give you

some literature to read about the second trimester and what to expect. I'm going to give you a prescription for prenatal vitamins. Make sure you take them with food or you'll get an upset stomach."

"What should I do about the throwing up? Should I expect that to continue?"

"Time will tell. Some women have morning sickness for months and others have it for a much shorter time. Buy some saltines and ginger ale. They should help to settle your stomach. You need to find an OB/GYN doctor too."

"Can you refer me to one? I don't know of any."

"I'll give you a few names and you can decide which one you want to contact." She types on the laptop some more, adding notes from my visit. She raises her head, glancing at me. "Tenley, I know this seems overwhelming and a little like the end of the world, but it's not. You'll get through this. Lean on the baby's father and let him be there for you."

If only it were that easy. Clancy and I aren't a couple. We're not even friends.

How are we going to raise a child together?

CHAPTER NINE

Tenley

Falling onto my bed, I sob into my pillow. How did this happen? We used a condom, and if it ripped wouldn't Clancy have told me?

I'm not very knowledgeable about pregnancy, but I realize my life is over as I know it. No more parties, no more drinking, no more dating. Not that I do a lot of any of those things, but if I wanted to, I could.

At least I would have options.

Rolling onto my back, I stare up at the white ceiling and run my hand over my flat stomach. God knows, it won't be this way for long.

Soon it will be like a mountain.

A massive mountain, and I won't even be able to see my toes.

I'm going to get fat.

Tears rain down faster at the thought. I know it's a silly way to think. But I like my twenty-one-year-old body. I've worked hard to look this way.

Fuck me. I'm too young to do this.

How am I going to afford a baby? I don't even have a job to make money and support a child. My child. Clancy's and my child.

Oh God. I'm having a baby with someone I barely know.

My phone chirps from inside my pocket and I ignore it. There's not a single person in this world or any other that I want to talk to right now. Grabbing a pillow, I hug it to my chest and roll to my side.

How am I going to tell my parents? They're going to be so disappointed in me.

Will they support me, or insist I give the baby up for adoption?

How will I tell Sophie?

God, she's going to say 'I told you so' and she's right. She did warn me away from Clancy. But this could've happened with anyone. We were safe and I'm still fucking pregnant.

What are the odds?

It's like a two percent chance.

I should've figured he'd have some super sperm that would find its way through the condom and knock me up.

And now I have to tell him he's going to be a father.

Clancy has big plans for his future and I'm about to blow them all out of the water. Unless he doesn't want to be a part of it.

Oh God, what if he doesn't want to claim our child?

This is overwhelming and I can't wrap my brain around it all. Everything will be fine, somehow. I don't know how, but it has to be.

It's too depressing and overwhelming to think of any other outcome. So that's what I'm going to keep telling myself until I finally believe it.

A knock on my door wakes me. My eyelids slowly lift and bright sunlight beams in my windows. Glancing at the clock on my nightstand I notice it's three in the afternoon. Rolling to my back, I groan, "Come in."

Sophie peeks her head in the door before stepping inside. "Hey, I've been texting you since yesterday morning and you never replied."

"I just saw you last night at the party."

"Tenley, it's Sunday. The party was two nights ago."

Oh shit. Have I really been asleep for that long?

I missed most of a whole day and didn't even realize it.

Is this what pregnancy does to you?

"I wanted to make sure you're okay."

"I'm fine."

"You don't look fine. In fact, you look horrible. Beautiful as always, but horrible."

"Thanks," I mumble into my pillow. The skin around my eyes feels puffy and tight from the deluge of tears I've cried. And I'm sure there's plenty more to come.

The news of me being pregnant hasn't even had time to sink in yet and now I need to tell Sophie.

Pushing myself up to a sitting position, I pat the bed next to me. "Come sit down. I need to talk with you."

She sinks down on top of the comforter. "What's up?" She looks concerned, and guilt assails me. I hope our friendship survives this conversation.

"When I woke up yesterday, I was really sick. I couldn't stop throwing up. I went to the doctor."

"I'm glad you went. Did they give you anything for the nausea?"

"No. I'm not sick. I'm pregnant," I blurt out. Might as well rip that band-aid off in one fell swoop.

Her eyes snap open comically wide, the whites showing all

around her irises. Except there's nothing amusing about what I'm telling her.

"You're pregnant?" she croaks.

Licking my dry lips, I slowly nod. "I am."

"How far along are you?"

"A little over three months, I think. I have to make an appointment with an obstetrician to find out for sure."

"Oh my God." She leans over, hugging me tightly. "Don't worry. Everything will work out in the end. I'll help you in any way I can."

Drawing back from Sophie's embrace, I meet her eyes. "You may not want to when I finish telling you everything."

"What's wrong?"

"Clancy is the baby's father."

"What?" her voice goes up an octave.

"Clancy is the father," I repeat, as if she didn't hear me the first time.

"Oh my God." Sophie shakes her head in denial.

"I'm sure it's his. I haven't been with anyone else in months."

"You were his wedding hookup?" she whispers.

It sounds so seedy now that she said it. But that's exactly what our time together was. Just a meaningless wedding hookup that will have us connected for the rest of our lives.

"Yes, it was me."

"Why would you do that? I've told you to stay away from him at least one hundred times."

I roll my eyes. "Do I really need to explain chemistry to you of all people?"

"What's that supposed to mean?" she huffs.

"You couldn't stay away from Miles and he was your professor."

"Yeah, but I was already in love with him before I knew he was my professor."

"I'm not saying you weren't. I'm making a point that chemistry can't be denied. Clancy and I both felt it and we made the decision to have sex. It's on both of us."

"Didn't you guys use a condom?"

"Of course we did, but it obviously didn't work properly."

"Ya think?" Sophie drolls, raising an eyebrow and I giggle.

I'm not sure why I find it so funny, but she starts to laugh along with me. It's the perfect tension reliever.

"You know I think you're a dumbass for sleeping with Clancy, but I'm going to support you in any way I can."

"I was hoping you'd still feel that way."

"Of course I do. You're my best friend. You were there for me with everything I went through to be with Miles. I'm not going to leave you when you need me the most."

"You don't know how much that means to me." My eyes tear up. "I don't know how I'm going to get through this."

"It'll be okay. You'll see."

"Sophie, I have to tell my parents. They're going to freak the fuck out."

"Do you want me to be there with you when you do?"

"Yes." I do want her to be there, but I shake my head. "No, you can't be. I got myself into this mess. I need to show them I'm not going to run from the situation."

"How are you going to tell Clancy? Are you going to call him?"

"I don't want to tell him on the phone. That seems so callous. 'Hey, how are you? Oh, by the way, you're going to be a father.'"

"I know my mom invited his family for Thanksgiving dinner. I can find out if he's coming."

"Yeah, at least if he's down here it would give me an opportunity to tell him in person. Do you think he'll want to be involved in the baby's life?"

"Clancy may be someone who avoids commitment, but

he's not the kind of guy to run from his responsibilities. And he loves kids. I'd be more concerned about him being involved more than you want him to."

"Honey, what are you doing here?" My mom gives me a quick hug and then looks me over with her standard critically assessing gaze. No matter how hard I try to hide things from her, she always notices when something's wrong.

"What's going on? You look tired."

"It's nice to see you too."

"Is that my girl?" my dad calls out, stepping into the kitchen. He wraps me in his comforting arms. I've always been a daddy's girl, much to my mother's disappointment.

"Hi, Dad."

"What brings you this way?" My parents live in a suburb of northern Virginia that's about twenty minutes from my apartment. It's far enough away that I don't stop by very often. My parents think I'm incapable of taking care of myself, and the conversation we're about to have will only solidify that sentiment.

"I need to talk to you guys about something." I gesture to the seating area. Silently, we all settle around the small, circular table.

I rub my hands together and my stomach tumbles uneasily, but there's no point in delaying the inevitable. "I'm pregnant."

Awkward silence fills the space until it's choking me.

My mother gasps. "You're pregnant?"

"Yes, I am."

"How did that happen?"

"I think we know the how of it, honey," my father interjects with a soft smile. He's always been the easier going of the two of them.

"You know what I mean." My mom sounds exasperated.

"It wasn't on purpose, if that's what you're asking," I reply.

"In this day and age how do you get pregnant unless it is on purpose?"

I try not to get angry, but her question is so ignorant. "Mom, we were safe and it didn't matter."

"I guess you weren't safe enough then. Why aren't you on the pill too? Two methods of birth control are better than one."

"If you must know, I don't have sex enough to make taking it worthwhile."

"The fact that you're going to have a baby negates that statement."

My dad rubs a hand over my mother's back. "Honey, calm down. Pointing the finger isn't going to help. Tenley has enough to think about. We need to help her, not make the situation worse."

Thank God for my dad. He's the steady one of the two of them. He'll be who I lean on when I need to.

"What are you going to do about school?" my mother asks in a calmer tone.

"I'm going to go for as long as I can. I think the baby will be due around the end of the school year, maybe a little before."

"Where will you live once the baby is born?" Dad inquires.

"I'm not sure. I don't have all the answers yet. I just found out I'm pregnant."

"Well, you better figure it all out. May is only six months away."

"I'm aware of that."

My father smiles consolingly. "Don't worry, sweetie, we'll

help you work all the details out. And you know you're welcome to stay here once the baby is born."

"Thank you. I appreciate that. I know you guys must be disappointed in me, but if it's any consolation, I'm more disappointed in myself than either of you could possibly be."

CHAPTER TEN

Clancy

THANKSGIVING HAS ALWAYS BEEN ONE OF MY FAVORITE holidays. I love every part of the meal, especially the mashed potatoes and stuffing. And this year my mom and I are in Virginia celebrating with her sister and her family. I don't mind because I'm hanging with Sophie and we've always been close.

Glancing at her across the table, I wonder how I can finagle a way to see Tenley. How do I broach the subject of her best friend without her growing suspicious? Is there a way for me to get her phone number without Sophie finding out?

Maybe I can suggest we go out and she'll happen to invite Tenley. I don't care how it happens, but I want to see her while I'm in town.

I shouldn't though.

I'd be smart to keep my mouth shut and stick close to my family. Seeing Tenley will only confuse my feelings and make it impossible for me to forget her.

Unfortunately, my dick doesn't seem to want to listen to reason.

"Do you want to come over to Miles' tonight? I'm having Tenley over too."

Wow. That was easier than I imagined. I didn't have to do a damn thing.

"Sure, I can do that. Where's Miles now?"

"He and Joey went to his parents' house. I wanted him to come here, but it's his mom's birthday tomorrow, so they're celebrating today."

"And you're okay being apart for the holiday?"

"We had all morning together and we'll be spending the rest of the day and night together, so a few hours apart isn't a big deal." She shrugs.

"You're not like most girls."

"What does that mean?"

"You're not clingy or insecure. I think a lot of girls would be upset if their boyfriend didn't come to dinner with them."

"Then you're right. I'm not like most girls because I'd never do that to Miles. He was the one struggling with being away from me today." She points to my plate. "Eat up. The sooner we finish, the sooner my mother serves dessert. Once that's done we can get out of here. You'll have a beer in your hand before you know it."

"Sounds good to me."

I ride with Sophie and she seems tense, but I don't know why. She insists things are great with her and Miles. If that's the case, why is she acting so strange?

He greets us at the door and pulls her in for a long kiss. I pass by them and head into his kitchen to grab a beer. I don't have an issue with making myself at home. It beats standing there watching my cousin play tonsil hockey with her boyfriend.

I find the bottle opener in a drawer and I'm popping the cap when they walk in. "Hey, Miles. How's it going?"

"Clancy." He tips his chin. "It's great to see you. Happy Thanksgiving."

"You too, man. How's life treating you?"

"Things are fantastic. What about you? How's hockey going?"

"I've been well, thanks. And the Terriers have been killing it on the ice. I think we're going to do great things this season if we can all stay focused. There's a lot of season left. I'm optimistic it will go as well as I hope, but who knows?"

The doorbell rings. "I'll get it." Sophie hurries off.

"How are you guys doing?" I question. I know what she's told me, but I want to get his take.

"We're great. You don't need to worry about Sophie, I'll always take care of her. She and Joey are my priorities."

"I'm glad to hear it."

"Hey, Miles," Tenley's husky tone wraps around me and she's not even talking to me.

"Hey. Happy Thanksgiving."

"You too." Her eyes skim across the distance, landing on me. "Clancy. How are you?" The sound of her saying my name affects me even more.

"I'm well. How are you doing?"

"I'm good, thanks." She sighs heavily, leading me to believe she's dealing with more than she's willing to reveal.

I take her in from head to toe and back up again. She's as beautiful as I remembered, but she looks tired. Is she struggling with school, or is it something else? Has some guy broken her heart and now he needs to be set straight? I'll gladly do it for her.

"Why don't you guys make yourselves comfortable in the living room and we'll be there in a few. I need to talk to Miles about a few things."

I nod at Sophie and then address Tenley, "Do you want a beer?"

"No, thanks."

"Want me to mix a drink for you? I know Miles has some good liquor stocked in his pantry. At least he did the last time I was here."

Miles laughs. "I still do and you're welcome to whatever you want."

Tenley shakes her head. "I'm fine. Let's go."

She walks in front of me and my eyes lock on her tight jeans, tracing over her heart-shaped ass. My hands twitch, the urge to grip those full curves is overwhelmingly intense.

Cock jerking in response, I look elsewhere. I can't get ahead of myself.

I don't even know if she's going to be on board for a repeat of what happened the last time I was in town. For all I know, she could have a serious boyfriend.

That would really suck.

She lowers onto the leather, choosing the end seat. I settle into the chair next to the couch and stare her way.

"You look tired." The words slip past my lips before I can stop them.

She glances side-eye at me. "Thanks. I'm glad I look like shit."

"Don't go putting words in my mouth. I didn't say that at all. You always look beautiful to me. You just happen to also look a little tired."

Her head tips forward, chin dropping to her chest. "Can you come sit here with me for a minute?"

Her question catches me off guard and confuses me, but I bound to my feet without hesitation. I move over, taking the seat next to her on the couch.

"Are you okay? You seem out of sorts." My eyes skim her

face, making note of the dark circles under her eyes and her pallid complexion. "Are you sick?"

Placing her back against the arm rest, she turns her body to face me and tucks a leg underneath her. Blue eyes lock on mine and never waver. "I need to tell you something and I don't know how to say it."

"I'm right here. I think the best way is to just get it over with."

She must have a boyfriend and she's feeling weird about me being here. Does she think I have expectations for us?

She inhales a ragged breath and her eyes shimmer as if they're filled with tears. What's going on?

"I'm pregnant."

The world stops on its axis. Lurching forward, I rise to my feet and turn to face Tenley. Wet trails of tears roll down her cheeks, falling off to make dark splotches on her purple sweatshirt.

"You're pregnant?" I question reflexively, my stomach knotting anxiously. She nods. "Who's the father?"

"You are," she raises her voice, crossing her arms over her chest.

How can she get angry with me for asking the question every man in this situation needs to ask?

If she didn't appreciate that one, she's really not going to care for the next question.

"How do you know it's mine?"

She springs to her feet, her finger already pointing in my direction. "I haven't been with anyone else but you."

Oh fuck.

Definitely not the answer I was hoping for.

Falling back onto the couch, I let my head lean onto the cushioned back. Scrubbing my hands up and down my face, I panic.

What am I going to do?

What is this going to do to my hockey career?

Before I cycle up too much, I need to get answers from Tenley.

Raising my head, I straighten up, doing my best to prepare for the rest of this conversation. "What do you want to do?"

She sits next to me. "I want to have the baby."

"Does that mean you want to give it up for adoption?"

"No," she snaps. "Do you want me to?" she barks the question out.

"No. I didn't say that. I'm only trying to find out where your head's at."

"Well, I can tell you adoption isn't an option for me. I know we're not together, but I still want to keep the baby. I don't mind if you don't want to be involved. I know you have plans that didn't include being saddled with a kid."

"Hey, I never said I didn't want to be involved." I place a hand on her leg. "Jesus, give me a few minutes to wrap my brain around this. You've known longer than me. When did you find out, anyway?"

"Last Saturday. I was feeling sick and couldn't shake it."

Shifting my weight, I turn to face her. "Why didn't you call me right away?"

"Did you really want me to tell you on the phone? Sophie mentioned you were coming for Thanksgiving. I figured this was the best option."

"Sophie knows?"

"Yes. She found out on Sunday when she came by my apartment."

"Who else did you tell before me?"

I'm annoyed I wasn't the first person she told since it's my child.

She rubs her lips together. "I told my parents."

"How did they take it?"

"My dad was more understanding than my mom, but on the whole, it went better than I expected."

I tuck a lock of dark hair behind her ear. My fingers trail down to her chin, tipping her face upward until our gazes merge. "When is the baby due?"

"The doctor I saw this weekend mentioned mid to late May. But she was just estimating. I need to find an obstetrician and they'll run blood work which will reveal a more reliable due date." She grips my arm and I release my hold on her chin. Her hand slides down my wrist to my hand and I slot our fingers together.

"When do you plan to do that? Wouldn't sooner be better than later?"

"It's on my checklist of things to do this weekend."

"Maybe I can help you choose one. We're in this together. I'm not going to let you go through this alone." I nod at her stomach. "That's my baby and I'm the only father he or she will ever have." I'm suddenly feeling territorial toward this kid I just found out about. It's amazing how quickly the parental instincts are kicking in.

"Okay. I'd like you to be involved. I don't want to do this alone."

I run my thumb over the back of her hand. "You'll never have to. I'll do whatever you need. I know I can't be here all the time, and most of this will fall on your shoulders, but I'm only a phone call away. I'd like for us to stay in touch daily. And I can get down here as often as possible."

"Thank you for not getting angry at me when I told you."

"Are you kidding?" She shakes her head. "How can I be mad when we're both responsible? We did the best we could by having safe sex. I guess the condom must've had a hole in it, because it sure as hell didn't break."

"Will you tell your mom?"

"Yeah, but I'll probably wait until we're back in Boston. I want her to enjoy the rest of her trip."

"Do you think she'll take the news that badly?" She looks concerned.

"No, I think she'll be excited about it in a weird way. She loves kids and always jokes about grandchildren. I guess I'll find out soon if she really wanted one or not."

"Will you tell the guys on your hockey team?"

"I don't know. I have a couple of close friends I'll probably share the news with right away. But the rest of them won't know until we get closer to the birth. I don't really like to put my business out there."

"I guess us living so far apart might be a blessing for you. No one will know unless you tell them. Me, on the other hand, I won't be able to hide it in another few months."

"Don't worry about what people will think. Who cares? We're having a baby and, yes, it's unexpected and less than ideal timing, but this little one will be loved like crazy. And they're the result of a phenomenal night we spent together. It might not be the ideal situation, but it could be a lot worse."

CHAPTER ELEVEN

Tenley

LYING ON THE TABLE, I THINK ABOUT CLANCY AS THE doctor examines me. Thinking about him helps take my mind off what she's doing between my legs. I hate going to the doctor and now I have a battery of appointments to look forward to for the next six months.

Clancy took the news so much better than I expected. I wanted to take back every negative thought I've ever had about him.

I basically informed him that his carefully laid out future is not going to happen the way he planned and he didn't freak out. If this situation doesn't bring out someone's true colors, I don't know what would.

Clancy is clearly a nice guy under that playboy exterior.

"Everything looks good. I want to do a sonogram to check the size of the baby. You're measuring at around three plus months, which is further along than most people I see for their first appointment. And according to your last menstrual cycle, your due date should be around the fourteenth of May."

That's right at the end of the school year. I wonder if I'll make it to my due date. I hope I can. Then I'll only have my senior year left. And if school doesn't fit into my schedule, maybe I can do some online classes, or at least go part-time.

I plan to finish my degree. It may take me extra time, but I'm committed to completing it.

"Will I be able to take a picture of the baby home with me?" I know Clancy is going to want to see what he missed out on.

"Yes, you'll get pictures you can keep." She smiles. "I'll send you downstairs for the sonogram now, so you can get out of here. I'm sure you have classes you need to get back to."

"I'm done for today, but I do have plenty of studying, with finals coming up."

"Don't overdo it. Make sure you get plenty of rest and take your prenatal vitamins and folic acid. I want to see you back here in four weeks for your next appointment."

"Okay."

"If you have any questions, you can call and speak to the nurse or leave a message for me. Take these pamphlets and read through them. I think you might find some of the answers to potential questions in there." She carries her laptop with her and exits the room.

I throw my clothes on and hurry out to the front desk to schedule my next appointment and check out. I jog down the flight of stairs instead of taking the elevator and head inside the radiology department. Reaching the desk, I give my name. I don't even make it to a chair before they're calling me inside.

"Hi, I'm Lisa and I'll be doing your sonogram." She gestures at the table and I lie down. "It says here you're thirteen weeks along."

I nod. "I am."

"Lie back."

I roll my shirt up and lower my pants to just above my

pubic bone, exposing my stomach. She tucks a towel around the edges of both pieces of clothing. She squirts clear gel on my skin and I wiggle, even though it's surprisingly warm.

She presses what looks like a small iron to my stomach, slowly moving it around until there's a thump, thump, thump repeatedly filling the air.

"That's your baby's heartbeat," she explains.

"It is?" My eyes go wide. I can't believe I'm listening to my baby's heart beating. Strong and fast, it's the most beautiful sound I've ever heard.

My eyes instantly fill with tears and I can't help but wish that Clancy was here to share this moment with me. Even if we're not together as a couple, we're still a team for this and I know hearing the heartbeat would mean as much to him as it does to me.

My eyes move to the screen and I'm blown away that I can see our child so clearly. I never expected to see a formed baby. I didn't think it would be so developed. He or she is waving their arms around and I swear I can already tell that the lips will look like Clancy's; full and well shaped. Tears blur my vision and I wipe them away. It's hard to believe this beautiful baby came from our night of hot sex.

The tech slowly moves the camera around, checking our little one's heart and spine to make sure they're developing correctly. "Everything looks great. I can't tell the sex yet, but there's only about five more weeks until you can find out. Do you think you'd want to know?"

Would I want to? "I'm not sure. I guess I can think about it in the meantime." And talk to Clancy about it too. Maybe he can even be here for the next sonogram.

The tech pushes some buttons and prints out a few different pictures for me to have.

"Oh my God. I love this. I get to keep these?"

She smiles at my excitement. "You do."

I can't wait to show Clancy. I imagine he'll be as surprised as I was at how developed the baby already is. I was expecting a nondescript blob, not little arms waving as if to say hello to its mommy.

"Hey, how are you?" Clancy's deep voice sends a shiver rocketing through me.

"I'm well. I'm calling because I had my first doctor's appointment today."

"You don't need to explain why you're calling me, Tenley. We need to be the best of friends if we're going to make it through this on the same page."

Best of friends?

Do I want more from him? It doesn't matter if I do because he's never going to be the relationship type.

"How did your appointment go? What did the doctor say?"

"She said everything looks good. I'm due mid-May."

"That's great. You might make it through the school year."

"That's the plan, but we'll see how I'm feeling at that point. I got to hear the baby's heartbeat when they did the sonogram."

"What's a sonicgram?"

"No." I laugh at his mistake. "It's sono-gram, not sonic."

"Whatever. Sonic sounds way cooler."

"If you say so. Anyway, a sonogram is like a black and white video of the baby. It shows a 2D image of them on the screen. The tech moved the camera over my stomach and we could see the baby moving. It was waving its little arms."

"You could see that it's a baby?" He sounds as surprised as I thought he'd be.

"Yep, I wasn't expecting that either. The tech printed out

some pictures for us. I'm going to send you pics of them. I can scan them into an email later if you want."

"Hurry up and send them so I can see." He's excited.

"Okay." Pulling up the images I took, I send them to him and wait for his reaction.

"That's our little one?" The words are whispered reverently.

"It is. Amazing right?"

"I can't believe how big the baby is already."

"Well, it's deceiving because it's actually tiny still, but the sonogram makes it seem bigger."

"Our kid's beautiful." His voice is laced with pride.

"I agree. I think he or she has your lips. Look at the pouty profile."

"As long as they don't have my propensity for foul language we'll be all set."

"We can put the kabosh on that right away. And you're going to have to watch what you say."

He sighs. "I know I am. I need to do a lot of things that I didn't expect."

I don't know why, but I find his words abrasive and annoying. He's got a lot of things to do that he didn't expect? What about me? I'm the one carrying a baby in my stomach for nine fucking months. I sure as shit wasn't expecting to be doing that any time soon. And I didn't plan on having a child with an acquaintance. That's for sure.

"I've gotta get going." I don't want to be on the phone any longer. I'm only going to get more aggravated. I need to remember that no matter how much he wants to be involved in this pregnancy, he'll never fully understand what it's like for me.

"Is everything okay?" he questions.

"Yeah. I have a lot of studying to do."

"No problem. I'll let you go. When am I going to talk to you again?"

"I don't know. I'll leave that up to you, I guess."

"I'll call you tomorrow. Don't work too hard. You need your rest too."

"Yes, Dad." I roll my eyes.

He chuckles. "I'm getting in some practice before the baby comes."

"Talk soon." I interject, wanting to get off the phone as quickly as possible.

"Sounds good. Bye."

Hanging up, I fall back on my bed. Dropping the phone on the mattress next to me, tears flood my eyes, trailing down the sides of my face. I don't even know why I'm crying. He didn't do anything wrong, really. Maybe it's because no matter how much he's involved, he's always going to be seven states away. All the responsibility of keeping this baby safe falls on my slim shoulders, and in this moment, I'm feeling every bit of the weight.

My chicken tastes so bland, I might as well be eating cardboard. I've always heard being pregnant made food taste better, but I've yet to experience that phenomena.

I haven't heard from Clancy for the past two days, even though he said he'd call. And I can't really blame him. He has the luxury of forgetting about the baby while he's at hockey practice or in class. Or maybe he's too busy partying with his buddies and a gaggle of girls. I can't really say because I don't know him well enough to be sure what he's doing. And I probably never will.

Regardless of all that, I'm angry he didn't follow through

on what he said. It doesn't bode well for the next six months-
- or the eighteen years after.

I'm struggling with keeping my head in a good space and it's difficult for me to maintain a bright outlook on anything. Is it because my hormones are changing? Or is it me being mopey and pathetic? I'm not sure, but either way, I don't have huge expectations for how we'll parent together. And no matter what, he'll most likely always be a part-time dad.

"What's up?" Sophie slides onto the chair on the other side of the table and aims a smile my way.

"Ugh, I'm in a bad mood. You might not want to sit here. I don't want to taint your sunny disposition with my shitty one."

She laughs. "As if you could."

Pursing my lips, I raise a brow. "Yeah, I forgot you're ridiculously happy with Miles and nothing can put a damper on it." I wouldn't have it any other way, though. I love how wonderfully he treats her and seeing her beaming smile warms my heart.

"I am happy, but I want you to be too. Tell me what's wrong, so I can help you."

Picking at my lunch, I shrug. "I don't even know. I can't really say it's from one particular thing. I think I'm just out of sorts and I don't know how to get over it."

"Oh jeez, it's probably your hormones."

"Shut up. I don't want to hear that as an excuse. Especially because you have no idea what it's like being pregnant. I'm tired all the time and, yes, I'm emotional. I hate it. This is not like me. It's like I've been possessed and I have no control over how I react to situations. Things that would normally not affect me seem like the end of the world. It sucks. If that's the hormones, they can fuck off."

"Hey, I'm sorry. I wasn't trying to piss you off. I only know that hormones are the big evil during pregnancy. My mother told me all about them. I think it was her way of scaring me off of having sex."

"Well, that plan was a fail." I giggle.

"Right? As if hormones are enough to keep a teenager from having sex. Hell, we deal with hormones every month already."

"I'm also a little bothered that your cousin hasn't called me in two days. He told me he would."

"Yeah, I figured this would be a problem at some point."

"What do you mean?"

"He's never had a girlfriend that he had to call daily."

"And he still doesn't."

"I know, but the reason I mentioned that, is he's never had a reason to call anyone on a regular basis. He probably doesn't even remember he's supposed to. I don't want to make excuses for him, but he's kind of clueless about this stuff. I'm sorry you're going to have to be the one to educate him on it."

"That's great. It must be nice to have the luxury of forgetting that you have a baby momma seven states away. And I won't be educating him on how to be considerate. I'll be too busy dealing with the pregnancy. If he's not going to be around much, I'd rather get used to it now."

"It's not that he's forgotten you. I'm sure he probably thinks about you throughout the day, but he forgets to call."

"I'm not going to make excuses for him, or allowances. I'm getting a crash course in responsibility whether I wanted it or not. And I can't forget about it, even if I wanted to. And let me be clear, I don't want to. I love this baby already."

"I know you do and he or she is lucky to have you. I know you'll be an amazing mother."

"Thank you. I needed to hear that. And coming from you it means a lot."

"I would never say something that wasn't true. You should

allow yourself time to get accustomed to the idea of having a baby. It's all still so new for you. You just found out less than two weeks ago and you've already been to the doctor."

"Speaking of that, I need to show you the pictures of the baby."

"Oh my God. You have pictures?"

Her excitement makes me smile as I dig through my bag and unzip the interior pocket. "Here, check these out." I hand over the small pieces of paper.

"I can't believe there's a little baby in there already."

"I know. It makes it all the more real."

"I bet. Oh damn, you know what I just realized. Your baby will be my second cousin." Sophie laughs and I join her.

"That's pretty bizarre to think about. It's kind of a mindfuck."

"It's actually awesome. We're going to be related."

"We're not going to be." I place my hand on my stomach. "But you and this little one will be."

"You're handling this whole situation so admirably. I don't know if I would be able to be so calm about everything."

"You'd be fine. You have Miles. To be honest, I don't feel like I'm calm. Maybe I appear so on the outside, but inside I'm a mass of worries."

"Everything will work out one way or another. Your parents will be there for you and so will Miles and I."

"Ah, but will Clancy?" I voice my concern.

"If I had to bet, I'd say yes. I know he didn't call you and you're angry about that, but you guys aren't a couple. Don't call him and see how long it takes for him to reach out. If it's more than another day or two, then I think you should blast him. And if you don't want to, I'll be happy to do it for you."

"There's no reason why he has to call me all the time. It's more for selfish reasons on my part. He's an integral piece of my support team. I feel less alone when we're in touch."

"There's nothing wrong with wanting to talk to him daily. Or at least a text to check in on you."

"I guess. I need to focus on me and the baby. Whatever Clancy decides his role will be, it will be. I can't make the decision for him."

CHAPTER TWELVE

Clancy

THE PUCK SAILS BY SHAW AND INTO THE NET, PUTTING Northeastern up by one goal. Fuck me. I didn't even see that coming, which is completely unlike me. But I can't keep my head in the game tonight.

As a defenseman, I'm like the quarterback on a football team. Staying calm and composed in the highest pressure situations is what sets a great defenseman apart from an average one. Usually unruffled and self assured, I can calm down the team and help them to focus. However, tonight, I'm thinking about my impending fatherhood more than the game we should be winning.

Focus. We need this win. My teammates and I have worked too hard to let the Huskies strip this victory from us. I'm going to do whatever it takes to make sure we get the win.

Five minutes later, we're still down by one when I race forward, blocking a shot that looked like a sure goal. I knew I could stop it. And Shaw, our goalie, can use a little help.

Keeping my head up at all times plays a big part in being able to see the play and identify the smallest seams to an open teammate, or the way to foil the opposition's play. My private skating coach has worked endlessly with me on handling the puck while keeping my head up. True play-makers don't need to look down.

Oliver raises an arm in celebration of my block, but it's short lived because we need to stay focused. Hockey games are won and lost in a matter of seconds all the time. And on any given day it can be your team to come out on the losing end. I'm just hoping that today it's the Huskies, and not the Terriers, who go home dissatisfied.

Oliver ties it up with thirty seconds left on the clock. Now's our chance to put this game in the win column once and for all. We've let them off too easy so far and we need to make up for it.

"Be aggressive, guys. We're almost done," I encourage, just before the referee blows his whistle. Donovan and one of the Huskies get in position around the red dot closest to the Huskies' goal to face off, positioning their feet on the hash marks. The player from the Huskies places his stick down on the ice before Donovan, while Oliver and I remain on the perimeter of the face-off circle, where the rules state we need to be.

The referee drops the puck between their two sticks. Donovan immediately draws the puck backward toward us. Skating forward, I receive the black disk, cradling it with my stick as I sweep it past the goalie and into the net. The crowd roars its approval and I raise both arms in the air, stick and all. We did it. Not the best win for us, but a victory just the same.

Arriving back at the house, I pull in to the driveway and groan. There's a party going on already and it completely slipped my mind. All I want to do is crash in my room and have some quiet time to think. But that's not going to happen now.

I've had my life turned on its head recently and I've barely had time to absorb everything. I feel bad because I haven't called Tenley for three days and I told her I would. I know we need to talk, but I'm not sure what I want to say. We're not a couple, or even friends, really. While I want to be friends with her and get to know her, the distance between us and my busy schedule will prove to be challenging. In fact, it already is.

I head inside the house, waving and nodding to the people I know before running up the stairs. My room is all the way at the end of the long hallway. Unlocking the handle, I slip inside and kick my sneakers off. I fall back on my bed with a sigh and stare up at the ceiling.

I can't believe Tenley is going to give birth to my child in less than six months. Most fathers have nine months to get adjusted to the idea, but not me. I must be special because it's less than six months from now. How will we have everything ready in time? It seems like an impossibly daunting task. I don't want to think about the details, but I need to.

Shit. I have to call Tenley. It's not fair for me to ignore her because I'm not sure what to say or do. She probably feels just as lost as I do.

Grabbing my phone from my pocket, I dial her number.

"Hello," her voice is a hoarse whisper.

"Hey. It's Clancy. Did I wake you?"

"Yeah. I fell asleep studying." I can hear her shifting positions.

"How are you feeling?"

"Tired." She giggles and I smile.

"Besides being tired, are you okay?"

"Yes. So far, so good. I'm getting hungry more often, but I haven't been throwing up, so that's a plus."

"That's a big plus. You must be relieved."

"I am. Morning sickness is no joke. I don't know how women make it through months of that. I hope I never have to experience it again."

"I owe you an apology." I scrub a hand over my face.

"What for?"

"I told you I'd call a few days ago and I never did."

"Why didn't you?" she asks, and I know for sure that she noticed. She must've been anticipating my call. Now I feel even worse for not following through.

"I was busy." Closing my eyes, I sigh. "That's not the whole truth. I didn't know what to say to you. I've been struggling with the news. It's still pretty fresh for me and it sucks because I can't do anything to help you. I'm on the sidelines watching, but I can't really help beyond emotional support. At least not on a steady basis. I can't move to D.C. and you can't move to Boston."

"I understand how you're feeling overwhelmed. I kind of sprang the news on you, but there wasn't really any way to tell you that would've been easier. Believe me, I thought about it."

"It's not about the way you told me. There is no easy way to say those words to someone."

"I appreciate you calling and being honest with me. We might as well tell each other the truth. What is lying going to accomplish?"

"You're right. I didn't call because I didn't know what to say. But I should've called and told you I was struggling, so you'd at least know I was thinking of you."

"Exactly. I can respect your position. I know you didn't want to be a father, and there's nothing wrong with saying that. Hell, I didn't want to be a mother either. All we can do is get through this the best way we can and be the best parents possible." She pauses as if she's gathering courage to say something else. "If you've had a change of heart about being involved in the baby's life, I'll understand. Well... I won't understand, but I can't make you."

She thinks I've changed my mind?

"No, I haven't. I want to be involved, but I'm not sure how to be when we're so far apart. There's so much you're dealing with and I can't do anything to help."

"Honestly, just talking with you is helping me. It makes me feel less alone."

"Good. I'll call you more often."

"I don't want you to think of calling me as a burden. You can text if that's easier."

"When's your next doctor's appointment?"

"In five weeks. We'll know the baby's sex after that."

"Are you having another sonogram?" I want to see the baby moving around instead of looking at pictures after the fact.

"I am."

"Can you text me the date, so I can try to be down there for it?"

"Sure. Why don't you get back to whatever you were doing before you called."

"I just got back from our game and there's a party going on."

"Well there you go." She harrumphs in my ear.

"You don't know what you're talking about. I came right to my room to get away from all the chaos. The game was a close one and I wanted to relax and unwind in peace. The moment I walked through the door, I knew that wasn't going to be possible."

"Now that you mention it, I can hear a dull hum of background noise on the line."

"Yep, that would be the bass and the hundred or so people that are here."

"I'm glad I don't have to deal with that. Especially now. I'd probably bite someone's head off."

"I might have to put an end to this party soon."

"Go have a beer and enjoy yourself. Don't keep all the girls waiting."

Does she really want me to hook up with someone else, or is this one of those tricks that women like to pull?

"They can wait. I think I'm going to skip the party."

"Thank you for calling. It means a lot to know that you care."

"I do." More than I should.

Coach pokes his head in the locker room. "Clancy, I'd like to see you in my office."

"Sure thing." I finish unlacing my skates and wipe the blades dry before slipping my sneakers on. I place my bag inside my locker cubby and rise.

"Dude, what do you think coach wants?" Oliver asks.

"I don't know. Hopefully, nothing's wrong." I shrug, feigning a nonchalance I'm not feeling. Could coach tell I was off my game the other night? We still won and I did stop a goal that would've tipped the win toward Northeastern.

Knocking on coach's office door, I wait for him to call me in before entering. The door closes behind me and he gestures to the chairs in front of his desk.

"Have a seat." He waits until I'm settled to continue. "I wanted to check in with you and see if you're okay. I've noticed you're not quite yourself lately." He holds up a finger to stop me from defending myself. "Don't get me wrong, your average play is still above most, but I can see that you're off. What's going on?"

I shrug my shoulders, unsure of what to tell him.

"You know that whatever you share with me in this room goes no further." I nod. "I can't help you if I don't know what's wrong."

Should I confide in coach? Will he think differently of me?

"Anything you tell me won't change my opinion of you," he answers, as if he read my mind. "Okay, that's not true. If you tell me snorting cocaine is your new favorite thing, I'm not going to be good with that."

I bark out a laugh, which I'm sure was coach's goal when he said such a ludicrous thing. "I can tell you I'm not snorting lines of cocaine or doing any other drugs."

"That's a relief."

Inhaling, I drag a deep breath in, exhaling on a long sigh. "I recently found out I'm going to be a father." The words spill from my lips.

"I take it this was unexpected?"

"You could say that. The mother lives in D.C., but she's from northern Virginia. She's best friends with my cousin."

"Is she your girlfriend?"

"No. I don't have time for a girlfriend, coach. You know how it is."

He presses his lips together, nodding. "I do. So, are you guys keeping the baby or giving it up for adoption?"

"You didn't say abortion as an option," I interject.

"No, I didn't think that would be something you'd be interested in."

"You're right. I couldn't live with myself if we took the easy way out at the baby's expense. We're going to keep it. Well, she's going to keep it and I'm going to figure out how to be there for them both. The distance between us feels enormous and insurmountable, like climbing Mt. Everest. It doesn't help that the news has barely sunk in."

"How did your mom take finding out she's going to be a grandmother?"

"I haven't told her yet."

"Clancy, what are you waiting for?"

"I don't know. I'm not ready to see the disappointment in her eyes."

"Maybe she won't be disappointed? It's not really fair for you to decide how she'll react. I've met your mom a few times now and she seems like a really cool lady."

"She is. You're probably right."

"Did you tell your father?"

"No. We're not in touch with him. He and my mom divorced years ago and I haven't seen him since."

"Try not to let anything distract you from your goals. Making the NHL would go a long way toward securing a better future for your child."

"Tell me about it. I can barely think of anything else."

"Then I want you to focus on your skating when you're on the ice. Make that the safe zone where nothing else seeps into your thoughts when you're playing. If they do, drive them back out. There's plenty of time for all the worry and contemplation when you're not at the rink."

I nod. "I'll do my best."

"I know you will. And if you need help with anything or just someone to listen, I'm here for you."

"I know you are, coach. Thank you. It means a lot that you care."

"You're one of my all time favorite players. I shouldn't tell you that, but what the hell. Maybe it will make you feel better. I know you have a great future to look forward to. Keep your eye on the prize when you're on the ice and everything will work out like we've planned."

CHAPTER THIRTEEN

Tenley

Christmas has come and gone, passing in a flash. Clancy has been calling or texting me daily. For the holiday he sent me a Boston Terriers long sleeve t-shirt and pajama bottoms with the hockey logo. They're ridiculously comfortable and I love knowing he picked them out. He also sent a onesie with the Terriers' hockey logo all over the material. I can't wait to see my son or daughter wearing it.

Today is my next doctor's appointment and Clancy is supposed to come with me. He's picking me up any minute now, or at least that's the plan. He said he was leaving at five a.m. and driving straight through. It's a seven hour drive on a good day. I'm not sure how long he can remain in Virginia for. I'm assuming he has to get back for practice or a game.

Sophie said he's staying with her at Miles' house, but he hasn't told either of us for how many days. And I haven't wanted to ask in case it came off as me pressuring him. That's the last thing I want.

I was going to offer for him to stay at my apartment, but where would he sleep? There's a couch he could use, but he's too big and tall. I'm not comfortable offering for him to sleep in my bed with me. Just because he knocked me up, doesn't mean I'm on board with any funny business. I have more self respect than that. At least I do when I'm not looking at him in person. Once he's here, I'm liable to forget my own name or swallow my tongue. Being in his company makes it difficult to think straight, which is how I got in this predicament in the first place.

I'm sitting on the front steps to my building when Clancy pulls up in his truck. He parks and gets out to open the passenger door for me. But before I can climb in he wraps me up in his arms.

"Hi. How are you?" He presses a gentle kiss to the top of my head. His tender gesture makes my stomach leap like a frog.

"I'm great. What about you? How was the drive?"

"It was surprisingly good. I didn't hit any traffic at all if you can believe it."

"That's pretty much unheard of. You better play the lottery if you're that lucky."

He places a hand on my back as I climb up into his truck. Closing the door once I'm situated, he hurries around and settles on the driver's seat. "Tell me where we're going."

"Falls Church. My doctor is at Inova Fairfax Hospital."

"I know where that is. You'll need to show me where to park, though."

Riding in silence for the first few minutes, I repeatedly flick my gaze his way. I can't get enough of looking at him. He looks hotter every time I see him. Damn, pregnancy hormones are a bitch when it comes to wanting sex. How am I going to keep my hands to myself? Especially when I can't forget how amazing our night together was.

"How was your Christmas?" He questions, tearing me from my lust-filled thoughts.

"It was nice. How about yours?"

"I enjoyed it, thanks. It was relatively quiet with my mom and me on Christmas Eve. I told her about the baby and she was excited."

"You just told her?"

"Yeah, I wanted it to be the right time."

"And Christmas Eve is that time?"

"Well, she didn't disown me, so I guess it worked out for the best. She actually told me she's excited."

"Your mom sounds awesome."

"Yeah, she is. There's not much she hasn't been through with me as a son."

"What did you do Christmas day?"

"My mom and I went to my grandparents' and she made me tell them about the baby too."

"Yikes. How did that go?"

"They took it well. I'm lucky; my family might not be large, but they're rocks when I need them to be."

"Maybe that's why you're so unflappable."

"What do you mean?"

"I told you I was pregnant and you didn't flip out. I blurted it out unexpectedly and you barely reacted."

"I was in shock."

"No, that's just the kind of guy you are. It's a great way to be."

"I'm glad you think so. I hope it will be helpful for you."

"It is. You calm me down and I need that."

"We're nearing the hospital. Where should I park?"

"If you take the next right there's a lot that you can park in and I can get the ticket validated when I check out."

I observe as Clancy backs his truck into an open spot. His large hands capably gripping the wheel, muscles in his forearms flexing attractively.

Shutting down the engine, he turns to me. "Don't move."

"Okay." What's this all about?

He closes his door and comes around to open mine. Holding out a hand, he helps me down.

"Thank you." That was a really sweet and unexpected gesture.

"My mom taught me well." He winks, ushering me toward the inside of the walkway, so he's closer to any traffic that might come by. I stare up at him with a curious expression on my face.

"What?"

"Did you want me to be on this side for some reason? Is it bad luck for you to walk here?"

His chuckle is deep and manly. "No, it's not about luck or anything besides keeping you safe. My mother taught me that as a man, I'm the protector. I'm supposed to walk on the outside and keep you safe."

"I've never had anyone do this before. I feel like I've been shortchanged."

"Well, you haven't dated anyone with manners then. It's a pretty basic concept. When our baby is old enough to walk, it will be the same thing. I guess it's a good thing you got knocked up by me and not some mannerless schmuck." He puffs his chest out.

I snort. "Yeah, as baby daddy's go, so far you're okay."

He stares pointedly down at me before he reaches for the door handle. " You haven't even begun to reap the rewards of me impregnating you."

I laugh out loud. I can't help it. He's so ridiculous. "By rewards do you mean the part where I gain copious amounts of weight? Or when my boobs get huge and achy? Maybe it's the part where I get the hungry horrors and want to eat everything in sight?" Stepping inside, I move down the hallway toward my doctor's office.

"No, it's not any of those things. I'll point them out when

we get farther along in this pregnancy. It's when I'll really earn my worth."

"I look forward to the big reveal."

"Think of it more as a subtle movement. Then your expectations will be less and you won't be disappointed."

"Gotcha."

Once I check in, I'm immediately called into a room. Clancy takes a seat in the extra chair, while I climb up onto the exam table.

The nurse takes my blood pressure and hands me a cup for a urine sample before she steps out of the room.

"Do you think they'd be able to tell if I gave them a urine sample instead of you?"

"What?" I shake my head.

"If I pissed in the cup instead of you, would they know? I'm just curious. I think we should try it and see if they do. Think of it as a quality control experiment. If they come back saying I'm x number of weeks pregnant, then we'll know they're full of shit."

I arch a brow. "Unless your urine changes once you knock someone up."

He studies me for a few heartbeats. Shaking his head, he smiles. "You had me going there, but what you said is impossible."

"You're right. It absolutely is, but I definitely made you wonder for a second or two." Sliding from the table, I pick up the cup and head into the bathroom. Once I'm finished, I set it on the back of the toilet and return to the room to find Clancy rifling through the cabinets.

"What are you doing?"

"Just checking what they have in here. Do you know how much money I could sell a prescription pad for?"

"Oh my God. Please tell me your joking and my baby's daddy isn't a common criminal."

He laughs. "What can I say? You're so much fun to fuck with. I can't help myself."

I situate myself on the table once more and glare at him. He sniggers and sinks down into the chair. The doctor knocks, entering the small room. The space seems tighter than last time and I know it has to be because of Clancy. Two-hundred-thirty pounds of man sitting in the chair takes up a whole lot of space.

"I'm Doctor Williams." She shakes his hand.

"Hey, I'm Clancy, the baby daddy."

I roll my eyes. Can't he just be normal and say his first name? Did he have to add the other part? It's self-explanatory.

"It's nice to meet you. I'm glad you're here with Tenley. She can use all the support she can get. Are you from this area?"

"No. I'm from Boston. I'm a senior at Boston University."

"Nice." She turns to me, dismissing Clancy. "How are you feeling now that you're nineteen weeks and well into your second trimester?"

"I feel better, less tired than I was."

"That should continue through this trimester. Why don't you lie down, so I can examine you."

I lower to my back on the crinkling paper. My eyes seek out Clancy at the far end of the room. He's watching intently.

Doctor Williams raises my shirt to just under my bra and takes out a tape measure. She feels my stomach and then measures from my pubic bone to the top of my uterus. "What are you measuring?" Clancy asks.

"It's called fundal height. It's used to reflect the size of the baby. By measuring at each appointment we can track that your baby is growing appropriately. During pregnancy the uterus grows. It starts out the size of an orange but it gets larger as time passes. Think of blowing up a balloon and watching it expand. That's what happens to the uterus."

"How's the baby's size?" Clancy asks.

"Right where it should be." I smile and notice Clancy does too. "You're scheduled for a sonogram. Do you want to find out the sex of the baby?"

"What do you think?" I raise my head.

"If the tech is going to know and it's going to be in your records, then I want to know too. Why should other people get to know and we don't?"

"Good point. I just want to find out so we can call he or she by their name."

I schedule my next appointment and lead Clancy down one flight of stairs. We enter the radiology department and I check in. They send me right back to a room. Hopping up on the table, I point to the chair next to me for Clancy to sit on. The tech comes in and I lie down. She pushes my shirt up to my breasts and squirts the warm gel on my stomach.

"Is that lube?" Clancy smirks.

"It's a water based gel that helps the sound waves travel properly. And this is the transducer. She places the small wand on my stomach, moving it around until our baby can be seen in black and white on the screen. The heartbeat thumps loudly through the speakers.

"What's that noise?" Clancy's eyes go wide.

"It's the baby's heartbeat," I answer. He beams.

"This is the baby's head, and the baby's heart. See the four chambers. Everything looks perfect. I see two arms and two legs."

"Look at them waving around. And those legs are kicking. Maybe our kid will be a soccer player," I mention.

"Hell no. I don't follow soccer."

"Well, I do."

"Let's see if we can get a view of what we're dealing with."

The tech moves the wand around for a different view and she smiles. "It looks like you guys are the proud parents of a little girl."

"A girl?" I gasp. I thought for sure with Clancy's super sperm I was destined to be the mother of a son. I already started to learn about hockey in preparation.

"We're having a daughter?" Clancy whispers in a choked voice.

Swiveling my head in his direction, I meet his gaze through my own blurry vision and nod. "A little girl. I can't believe we're having a daughter." I was envisioning a future with no more pink or purple, but now I can load up on it. I can't wait to shop for some little clothes. I notice the smile fade from Clancy's lips. "What's wrong?"

"I was thinking about how much work having a daughter will be."

"And having a son would be easier?"

"My mom always said 'little girls bring trouble home while little boys bring trouble to other people's houses.'"

"What does it matter if there's still trouble?"

"I don't know. It doesn't. All that matters is she's not dating until she's twenty."

I smile. She's already got her daddy worried for her safety. It won't take her long at all to wrap him right around her finger.

CHAPTER FOURTEEN

Clancy

OH LORD, WHY ME?

Why do I have to be the father of a daughter?

And to make matters worse, her mother is drop dead gorgeous and I imagine she will be too. I'm so screwed. I see guns in my future. Lots and lots of guns.

Glancing back at the screen, I grin when I notice her little arms waving around as if she's happy. Does she know her mommy and daddy are here watching her?

A lump the size of a golf ball settles in my throat as I fight off tears. I'm a big, tough hockey player and all it takes to make me cry is finding out I'm the father of a little girl.

Can she feel how much we already love her? I hope she can. I never want her to doubt our love for one second. No matter how hard Tenley and I try, we will make mistakes. There's no way we can't. But our daughter will never doubt how much I love her, and I can already tell that Tenley will be a wonderful mother.

The tech prints out pictures for us and wipes the gel from Tenley's stomach. We thank her and she walks out of the room, giving us some time alone.

Tenley sits up, wiping the wetness from underneath her eyes. I rise and step closer to the table, drawing her forward into my arms.

"Thank you." My voice is a gruff whisper.

"For what?" She hugs me tighter.

"For our daughter. She's perfect already."

"We made her together."

"I know we did, but you're the one who's taking such amazing care of her. I'm sorry it has to be all on you until she's born. Although, I can't think of a better person for the job."

She wiggles closer to me and I'm guessing she doesn't even realize she's doing it. My nose nuzzles her long, dark hair, drawing in the fresh, floral scent of her shampoo. It's the same one she used the night of the wedding. My dick reacts and I draw back.

"We should get going. I'd like to take you to dinner, if that's okay with you."

"Sure. I'd love to go to dinner with you. As a matter of fact, I'm starving."

"I've never been here before, have you?" Tenley curiously scans the interior of Bub's Pub.

"I stumbled upon it one night when I was visiting my cousins."

"Do you mean you stumbled in? Or stumbled out?"

I laugh. "I didn't do either. Finding it was a lucky break. I was killing time and decided to check out their menu. The food's awesome and I've been back a few times since."

"I like the Irish feel of the decor. The dark wood and dim lighting are welcoming. I feel like I could be sitting in some pub in Ireland."

"I think that's probably the idea of the Irish themed decor," I droll.

"You think?" she teases back. "What's good to order?"

"I've only tried a couple of different things. The Shepherd's Pie is awesome and the steak tips and mashed potatoes are mouth watering. I've also had the chicken tenders and potato skins."

"That's more than a couple."

"You felt the need to point that out, huh?" I smile and she tips her head to her shoulder in a half shrug.

The waitress stops beside our booth to take our order. I get the Shepherd's Pie and Tenley gets mac and cheese with chicken tenders.

"Mmm, I'm so hungry. I can't wait to eat."

"Do you always have a healthy appetite, or is it because you're eating for two?"

"I can put food away surprisingly well. I think people are deceived by my size."

"I hope you ordered whatever you want. I don't want you to eat less than you should because you're worried about me seeing how much you eat."

"Yeah, that would never happen. You're going to see so much worse by the end of this pregnancy. I don't think it matters how much I eat in front of you. Besides, we're just friends, right?"

Is she trying to remind me that we'll only be friends? Or am I way off base?

I don't know what to say in reply. Mostly, because I need to analyze my own feelings for her and I don't want to go through the work. Do I find her attractive? Yes. Would I fuck her again if I had the chance? Hell yes. In a heartbeat. Do I want her to be more than a friend? I'm not sure. I don't think of her like I do my female friends. She's important and I enjoy her company more.

What that means I'm not ready to work out. So, I answer in the only safe way I can. "Sure, we're friends."

"Friends tell each other things."

Oh here we go. The let's confess shit we don't want to discuss. Every female I've ever tried to be friends with always has to turn things awkward by asking too many questions.

"Friends tell each other *some* things," I correct.

She grins mischievously. "How many girls have you been with?"

I don't answer right away. I don't know the number off the top of my head. And I might forget a few just because they were meaningless hookups. I decide to fuck with Tenley a little. I flip each of my fingers on both hands up one at a time until I run out of fingers.

"Okay, can I borrow your fingers to count too?"

Her mouth drops open. "You need mine too?" she squeaks.

"Yep. I might need your toes too."

"Oh gross. Don't tell me this after I've already slept with you."

I laugh and brush my hair back from my face. "I only need a few of them."

"Thirteen is your number?"

"Yep. I think I got them all."

"I was lucky thirteen," she states.

"That's one way to look at it. I guess it depends on what your version of lucky is."

"Well, I'm past the point of thinking of this pregnancy as a curse and I'm accepting it for the blessing it is. The timing sucks, but you can't have everything." She shrugs.

Tenley is amazing. She has such a great outlook about our situation. Any other girl would probably be freaking out and blaming me. And she's looking on the bright side.

"Don't you want to ask me what my number is?"

Do I really want to know how many guys she's been with? Hell no. I shake my head. "Not really."

"I'm going to tell you anyway. It's four, including you."

"That's a low number."

"I'm only twenty-one."

"Damn you're a slut," I tease.

"Shut up."

The waitress drops off our food, barely setting our plates down before we both dig in. She forks a large pile of macaroni and cheese into her mouth with a moan. "This is so good. I'm going to inhale this meal."

Watching her eat is already testing my resolve and we're only one bite in. She closes her eyes with the next two bites, wrapping her red lips around the fork and my pants feel tighter by the second.

"I'm glad you think so. We can come back here whenever I'm in town." *If you promise to moan and lick the fork, I'll make sure I'm here weekly.*

"I don't want you messing up your hockey future because you're coming to visit too often. We can keep in touch on the phone just fine."

"I want to be here and I'll come as often as I can. There will be times when I can't be there, but I'll always do my best."

"I love that you came to the appointment with me today and got to see our little angel, but you have to think about your future. This baby is only one part of it."

"She's a big part of it," I clarify.

"I know she is, but you have a whole life back in Boston without us. And you always will. And who knows where you'll end up once you're picked up by a team."

What is she saying? Does she want me around or not? I thought we were in a good place, but now I feel like she's wishing I wasn't here.

We settle into silence as we demolish every bite on our plates. My thoughts are a jumbled mess. All the progress I thought we'd made recently now feels unsure. I thought I had solid footing under my feet, but now the ground feels shaky and uneven.

"Would you mind meeting my parents sometime?" Her question catches me off guard.

"No. We can do that whenever you'd like. I don't have plans now that your appointment is over."

"When do you have to go back?"

"The day after tomorrow. I need to leave around five a.m. to make it home in time for my hockey practice." I don't tell her how I should leave tomorrow because I'm missing practice and gym time. Coach excused me from today's and tomorrow's, but that's the best he could do.

"If you need to leave sooner it's okay," she offers.

"Do you want me to leave?" I spit out the question. She keeps mentioning me leaving and I don't want to stay when I'm not wanted.

"No." Her eyes widen with surprise. "Why would you think that?"

"Oh, I don't know. Maybe because you keep mentioning me leaving or telling me I can go. You're giving me a complex."

"I'm sorry. I don't want you to leave. Having you here is reassuring for me. I know that I'm not alone in this."

"You're not alone, even when I'm at home. I'm only a phone call away."

"I know, but having you here is better. I think I'm overcompensating because I don't want to be a burden for you."

"You're not, though. And if you keep telling me to leave I'm going to take you up on it because I'm not overstaying my welcome."

"I want you here. I promise."

"Okay, now that we got that out of the way, what do you want for dessert?"

"What makes you think I want dessert?"

"Come on. I watched you eat every bite of that without pause. And you didn't even settle back into the seat like you were trying to digest."

"Damn, you're good." She giggles. "I absolutely want dessert, but I was going to settle for ice cream at my place."

"You can still have ice cream later, but now you can have that brownie sundae I saw you eyeing at the table next to ours."

She drops her chin to her chest, shaking her head from side to side. "Oh God. Do you think they noticed?"

"Well, it was kind of hard to miss the trickle of drool running from the corner of your mouth."

Her head snaps up, her mouth in an O. "I wasn't drooling." I arch a brow at her. "Okay, maybe a little." She lifts one shoulder in a sheepish shrug.

I laugh. She's adorable and I love teasing her.

Raising my arm, I flag down our waitress. "Can we please get one brownie sundae and a slice of apple pie with vanilla ice cream?"

She nods. "I'll be right back with those."

"I got pie too, in case you want both."

She rolls her eyes. "Clancy, I'm eating for two, not four."

CHAPTER FIFTEEN

Tenley

My eyes flick toward Clancy in the passenger seat of my car. "Are you sure you don't mind coming to a party with me?"

"Not at all. "

"You don't think it's pathetic that I'm pregnant and I still want to attend a party?"

"Why would I think that? I'm interested in checking it out. Maybe I'll get to pound in the faces of a few of King University's hockey team members." He cracks his knuckles just by opening and closing his fists.

"Don't even think of it. I have to go to school with these people."

"Yeah, and you have to raise a child with me. Whose side are you going to take?"

"Okay, good point. But I still have to go to school with these people, and you won't be around to defend me all the time so..." I let the rest of the sentence hang in the air.

"So, I should only beat one face in?" I can hear the amusement in his tone and I realize he's teasing me.

"It's not nice to stress out a pregnant woman."

"Fine. Ruin all my fun why don't ya."

"Hey, you ruined mine," I toss out flippantly. And he doesn't reply. I glance side-eye at him, but his head is turned toward the passenger window.

"Clancy, you know I'm only joking, right?"

I feel his eyes on me. "Are you? It doesn't seem like a joke when it could be the truth."

"I really am. I know you didn't knock me up on purpose. And if I could go back and do things differently, I wouldn't. This baby wasn't planned, but I already love her more than anyone or anything."

Stopping at a red light, I turn to him. Our eyes meet and his are more earnest than I've ever seen.

"I wouldn't change anything either. I can't wait to hold our little girl in my arms."

My heart flounders inside my chest. I picture the giant of a man beside me holding our tiny baby. Swoon. I think I just fell a little in love with him.

Okay, I fell a little *more* in love with him.

My heart didn't come out of the night we spent together completely unscathed. He stole a piece of it and now he's gotten hold of another.

How long will it take before there's nothing left to give to another man?

Will I spend the rest of my life pining for Clancy, the one guy I can't have?

"Tell me who I'm going to meet at this party." He changes the subject and I'm grateful. My mind was going down a path that leads to nothing but negative thoughts and worrying about things I don't need to be.

"You'll meet my other best friend, Cassie. She's a hoot. I think you'll like her."

"What does she think of us having a baby?"

"She's been supportive. No one can compete with how awesome Sophie has been, though. She's a rock."

"Any ex-boyfriends going to show?"

"Maybe. I can't say for sure. Why?"

"No reason."

"Well, if you must know, one of them is on the hockey team and he lives at this frat."

"So, are you a puck bunny?" He flashes a grin so wide I catch the white beaming in my periphery.

"Fuck you. I'm not some groupie chick who waits around for a guy's attention. Did it ever occur to you that maybe he waited around for me?"

"Are you saying you collect guy groupies? Do you put them in the 'Ten Pen?'"

I laugh so hard I snort. "Ten Pen? That's hilarious. How do you think of this stuff?"

"I'm just blessed."

"Is that what they call it?"

"I'm blessed in many ways," he reiterates, and I can't disagree. After all, I've got firsthand knowledge of exactly how well he is blessed.

The party is in full swing when we arrive, but that's no surprise. King University frat parties always get rowdy and crowded.

"What do you think?" I glance up at Clancy beside me.

He shrugs, unimpressed. "It's a party."

"Right. You've seen one, you've seen them all. Come on. We can grab you a beer in the kitchen." I point toward the back of the house.

As we progress toward the kitchen, I notice every girl's eyes landing and lingering on Clancy. Gritting my teeth, I fight the urge to shout 'back the fuck off.' I want to place a proprietary hand on him just to claim him as mine. He's fresh meat for all these girls.

The students at King University don't look like Clancy. He's like a hairy giant with his shoulder length blond hair and thick beard.

Most of the guys I go to school with are clean shaven and their clothes scream money. They get haircuts every two weeks.

Clancy, on the other hand, oozes machismo and bad boy, like sweat coming out of his pores. In his jeans, flannel shirt, and work boots, he has an I-don't-give-a-shit-what-I-look-like way about him that draws attention like a flashing neon light. And he's ten times more attractive than any of these guys could ever be; my ex included.

We find the fully stocked cooler in the kitchen. Clancy grabs a beer for himself and a bottle of water for me.

"Thank you. You might as well enjoy yourself. I'm your designated driver for the night."

"I won't be drinking more than a couple of these anyway. I'm in enemy territory. I've gotta keep my wits about me in case I need to kick some King ass."

"Do you get in fights that often back home?"

"No. Because everyone knows who I am and they also know not to fuck with me."

"Well, don't start any trouble here. You have to set a good example for our daughter. Tonight can be considered the first practice toward it. You have five and a half months to perfect the ability to let shit roll off of you."

He raises his beer to his lips, taking a deep pull. I watch his neck as the muscles contract while he swallows.

"Shit doesn't roll off of things. It sticks, and I'm not the type to ignore it. I probably never will be. Our daughter will never know that unless someone tries to mess with her or you in front of me. And if they do, she'll see firsthand how her father takes care of assholes who bother the people I care about."

Does he really care about me? My stomach somersaults at the thought.

"Hey." My roommate sneaks up on me.

"Hi. Cass, this is Clancy." I place my hand in the middle of his chest. His heart beats strongly under my palm.

"Clancy, this is Cassie." My hand slips down to his ribs before falling back to my side. He's solid as a rock, just like I remember.

They shake hands and exchange pleasantries. I hoped these two would hit it off.

"Have you seen Harry yet?" she mentions my ex.

"Uh-uh. I haven't seen him in months, though."

"He looks good."

"I'm sure he does, but he's still an asshole at heart." I caught him kissing another girl when we were together. I'm lucky that's all they were doing at the time. If they had been naked, I'm not sure what I would've done.

"Is Harry the ex who plays on the hockey team?" Clancy inquires.

"Yep, the one and only," Cassie is quick to reply.

"Be sure to introduce me to him." Clancy's eyes gleam mischievously.

"Not happening." I stare sternly at him.

"I'll see what I can do," Cassie offers with a wink.

"Don't help me out any," I add.

We adjourn to the back deck to get away from the crush of bodies, but there's a fair share of people outside too.

"Hey, Tenley." Reid comes over and gives me a hug. "How are you?" he asks as he steps back.

"I'm great, thanks."

"Who's this?" Clancy practically growls the question.

I aim a *behave* at him with my eyes. "This is Reid, a friend of mine."

"And mine," Cassie chimes in, smiling at Reid. He doesn't notice.

Clancy nods.

"It's nice to meet you." Reid is quick to make him feel welcome.

"You play hockey?" Clancy asks.

"Nah, man, I'm on the football team. Do you?"

"Yeah, I play for Boston University."

"Ah, the Terriers." Reid turns to me. "Is this the guy you meant when you mentioned knowing someone on the Terriers?" Thankfully, he doesn't repeat the rest of what I said.

"I can't remember," I lie.

Clancy grins crookedly. "You were talking about me?"

"Don't be so happy about it. If I was, chances are it wasn't good."

"Good, bad, it makes no difference to me. I just like knowing you were thinking of me when I wasn't around."

"Reid, Clancy is Sophie's cousin."

"You're friends with Sophie?" Clancy crosses his arms over his chest.

So, he's protective with everyone he cares about. This information only makes him more attractive to me.

"Reid had a crush on Sophie, but he's realized nothing's going to come of it."

"Hey. You never know," he fires back, but I can tell he's joking.

"Dude, I have more chance of winning the lottery than you do of Sophie and her boyfriend splitting," Clancy informs him.

"I'm glad she's happy. Tenley is usually the only one who gives me shit for liking her."

"I can't help it. You need to open your eyes to who else is

around. You might miss out on something great while you're pining for Sophie." I glance at Cassie and back to Reid, but he doesn't notice.

Jeez. Do I need to spell it out for him? How can such a good looking, popular guy be so clueless? Cassie is crazy about him. She hasn't even told me and I can tell. Hell, it's not like she's trying to hide it. At this point everyone but Reid must know. The only way she could make it more obvious is if she wore a shirt announcing it. And even then, he still might not notice.

"I'm going to grab another beer. Anyone need anything?" Reid asks.

I hold up my still almost full bottle of water and shake my head.

Cassie edges closer to his side. "I'll come with you. I'm not sure what I want."

We watch them walk away and then our eyes connect. "Cassie has it bad." Clancy slowly ticks his head from side to side.

"She does," I agree. "What did you think of Reid?"

"He seems like an okay dude for an Ivy Leaguer."

"He really is."

"Point out your ex to me. I promise I won't beat his ass." He leans forward until his lips are almost brushing my ear. "I want to see who might've been your baby daddy if I hadn't filled the vacancy." His breath fans across my skin and it's all I can do to keep from trembling.

"You're an asshole," I whisper harshly. "You make it sound like I got knocked up on purpose."

"Come on, I'm messing with you. We both know that's not the case. The condom was mine."

"Are you sure you didn't poke a hole in it to latch yourself to me for the rest of your life?" I jest.

"I probably shouldn't have used a condom from two thousand fifteen," he deadpans, and I giggle.

"There's no way you'd have one that old. I'm sure you used them all up."

"All joking aside, I'm always careful. And I definitely wouldn't keep expired condoms. Now, stop stalling and point out Harry."

CHAPTER SIXTEEN

Clancy

Tenley's head pivots from side to side as she looks around the deck. Staring up at me, she tips her head to the left. "See the guy in the King hoodie?"

"The pussy-looking one?"

"Oh my God, stop it. He's a decent guy. It just didn't work out with us."

"Why'd you break up?"

"I caught him sucking face with someone else."

"Yeah, he sounds like a real nice guy. It's good you feel the need to defend him."

"I don't, usually, but I don't want you to go talk to him."

"Can I go punch him for breaking your heart?"

"He didn't break my heart. I wasn't that into him and he did me a favor. He did you one, too, because if he and I were still a couple, I'd have never had sex with you. So think about that."

I press my lips together. "Hmph."

"What's that?" Tenley cups her ear. "You don't have anything to say?" I shake my head. "I need to mark this day down on my calendar."

"Did you make a note of the day we slept together?" He leans forward, studying my expression.

"No. Don't be silly."

She has an oh-shit-I-did-mark-it-down-on-my-calendar look on her face.

I grin. "Did you break out your diary and write about our time together?"

"How do you..." She stops herself from saying any more, but I already have her number.

"Did you write #dreamsdocometrue? Did you describe my body in explicit detail?"

"No," she shouts, her cheeks pinkening.

"I bet you even did a crude drawing or two." I wiggle my brows lecherously. Her icy eyes pop wide open and I know everything I'm guessing is true. "I think you're lying, but I don't know why you think you need to."

"Maybe because it's embarrassing as fuck and I can't stand to see you gloat. You're always right, dammit. It's not fair." She barely contains herself from stomping her foot in aggravation. And that I'd love to see.

"Did my ears play a trick on me, or did you just admit I'm never wrong?"

"I'm pleading the fifth." She purses her lips temptingly.

I bark out a laugh. "Of course you are." Raising the beer to my lips, the cool liquid rolls into my mouth, quenching my dry throat as I swallow it down. I tip the lip of the bottle toward Tenley. "I'm going to be the nice guy I am and let you off the hook, for now."

"Gee, thanks."

"Hey, Tenley. How are you?"

My head snaps toward the voice. "Harry. I'm good. How about you?"

"No complaints. Can I talk to you for a minute?" He

hooks his thumb over his shoulder toward an empty corner of the deck.

"Uh..." she stumbles.

"She's busy right now," I answer for her.

Harry scowls. "And you are?"

"I'm the guy she's upgraded with." I place my beer bottle down on the railing, crossing my arms over my chest. The flannel material of my shirt hugs my flexed biceps so tightly I'm surprised it doesn't shred. I'm angry like the Hulk.

"Congratulations. I wish you guys the best." Harry scurries away.

"I'm annoyed I ever dated him," she confesses.

I wrap an arm around Tenley. "See? He's a pussy, just like I said."

Tenley slides onto the passenger seat before I can get out of the car and open her door.

"Hey. You're supposed to let me be a gentleman."

"I know, but one time won't kill you. It's cold out there. I wanted to get warm as soon as possible."

"Do you need me to turn the heat up?"

"No. This is wonderful. I should've dressed warmer. I underestimated the chill in the air. I shouldn't have, we are in January."

"What's the plan for today? What do you need to do while you have me here?"

"Don't hate me for this, but I told my parents we'd swing by for a quick visit. I said you had to head back home today, so we won't get stuck there."

"Sure. Does that mean we're going there now, or later?"

"Fuck it. Let's go now and get it over with. You might

have to cheer me up when we leave there. No one can put me in a funk like my mother."

"No problem. I bet I can make you forget all about her." If I could do what I wanted to her, I'd make her forget her own name. But now's not the time.

I'm not sure there will ever be a right time for us. We may be destined for a great friendship and no more romance. Only time will tell for sure. I'm not going to pressure her into sex and have it backfire on me. She could get pissed off and refuse to let me be involved in the baby's life. Then it would turn into a messy legal matter. We'd be at odds, and no one wants that.

Tenley directs me to her parents' place. I park my truck in their driveway and stare up at the large brick house, typical in the northern Virginia suburbs.

"Did you grow up in this house?"

"Yep. My parents bought it when my mother was pregnant with me."

"It's nice. Looks like a great place to grow up."

"Thanks, it was."

"Will you move back in with them once the baby is born?"

"I'm not sure. I don't want to, but I might have to due to finances. Also, I know my parents will help me out taking care of the baby. I can't stay at the apartment I'm at now. It wouldn't be fair to expect my roommates to want to, or have to, deal with a baby all the time."

"Right."

I want to tell her not to worry. If I get offered a contract, I'll be paying for everything and she can have her own place. And if I don't, I'm still going to contribute my fair share.

I help her down from the seat and keep my hand on her back all the way to the front door.

Once we step inside, my gaze wanders around the elegant

decor and I feel underdressed in my black fleece pullover and jeans.

I wish I'd known she planned to introduce me to her parents today. I would've worn a button down shirt at the least and fastened my hair back in a ponytail, giving the illusion of short hair.

I could've trimmed my beard too. Right now I look more like a lumberjack and less like a college student with a three point eight grade point average.

"Mom, Dad," Tenley calls out as we move through the downstairs. Our steps echo through the open space. Should we have taken our shoes off? I'm second guessing myself a lot right now, which is unusual for me. But these are Tenley's parents and it's important they like me. I'm going to be tied to them for the next eighteen years at the least. And if they don't approve of me, what will it do to my relationship with Tenley?

"Tenley, dear. How are you?" Her mother holds her arms out and draws her into a hug.

"Hi, Mom. This is Clancy, the baby's father."

"Mrs. Davenport, it's wonderful to meet you. I can see where your daughter gets her beauty from."

Her mother smiles while Tenley stands next to her rolling her eyes. She holds her arms out toward me. "I'm a hugger," she mentions.

"Since when?" Tenley mutters.

I step forward into an awkward hug, gently patting her back. As I pull away, Tenley's father wanders over.

"Daddy," she beams and rushes into his arms. I can already tell who her favorite parent is.

"How's my girl? Are you feeling okay?"

"I'm well, and yes, I am. I want you to meet Clancy, the father of your granddaughter."

"Granddaughter?" her mother gasps.

"Clancy, it's wonderful to meet you. I've heard good things about you from Tenley."

"Really? I'm surprised she has anything nice to say about me at all," I joke.

Tenley whacks me across the chest. "Oh stop. You know that's not true."

"How long have you known about the baby's sex?"

"We went for the sonogram yesterday," Tenley explains.

"And we're just finding out now?" Her mother seems annoyed we didn't share the information sooner.

"Mom, we've been busy since and got over here as soon as we could. Jeez. How about a thank you for coming?"

"Thank you for bringing Clancy by. We've both been hoping to get acquainted with the father of our grandchild. Why don't we go sit down and get to know each other?" Mr. Davenport suggests. He leads the way into the living room and we pair off sitting on the two couches facing each other.

"Tell us about yourself." Her father gestures at me.

"I'm a senior at Boston University. I play on the hockey team and I do well in school."

"Clancy's being scouted for the NHL. Everyone says he'll make it."

"Excellent. How did you two meet?" Mrs. Davenport asks.

"Clancy is Sophie's first cousin," Tenley answers with a smile.

"Well isn't that something?" her dad comments.

"We've known each other for years," I explain.

"What are you going to do about the distance between you when the baby comes?"

"Mom, we have months to go. We'll work out the details later."

"It's easy to say that, but time passes faster than you think it will. Before you know it, you'll be scrambling to figure it all out."

"If that happens, we'll deal with it then." I can tell Tenley is getting upset and that's not good for her or our daughter. Shouldn't your elders calm you down, not add to your concerns? That's how it works with my mom.

"I hate to cut our visit short, but I have to get back to Massachusetts. It's a long ride and if I don't leave soon I won't make it on time." I rise and Tenley jumps to her feet beside me. "It's been wonderful meeting you both. I look forward to getting to know you more the next time I'm in town."

Handshakes and hugs are exchanged all around. I catch Tenley's hand, giving it a gentle squeeze, letting her know it's time to go. We move to the foyer with her parents following us. Her hand in mine feels so natural, as if we've done this hundreds of times. But that's what being with Tenley is like. We fit together comfortably. I don't have to try to impress her. I can be myself, and I like to believe it's the same for her.

Once we're outside and the door is closed behind us, I pause and turn to face her. "I hope you don't mind that I stepped in and said we had to leave."

Her stormy eyes stare up at me settling to a calm blue. "No. God no. It was perfect."

"You looked like you were getting upset and I don't want anyone or anything to make you worry." Raising my hand, I cup her cheek. "Everything will work out fine. You have no reason to be stressed."

She nods and I notice her eyes shining with a sheen of tears. She presses her lips tightly together and looks down. I know she doesn't want me to see her cry.

I raise her chin with my index finger, but she still avoids my eyes. "Look at me."

Her gaze slowly raises until I can see her tear-filled stare. "I mean it. I know you're scared at how much is still up in the air, but one way or another we will get through this. Together.

I'm not going anywhere. I'll be with you every step of the way. You need to stay calm and trust me." She nods, but it's not convincing. "I mean it. Can you trust me?"

"Yes," she whispers and my chest tightens to the point of pain. I'm overcome with emotions I've never experienced before. I'm the one who should be scared. She makes me feel things I don't want to. And I can't seem to stop it from happening. And the hardest part is, I'm not sure I want it to stop. Ever.

CHAPTER SEVENTEEN

Clancy

AFTER SPENDING A COUPLE OF DAYS WITH TENLEY I FEEL
better about everything. I'm confident we can find a way to
co-parent without killing each other.

It's dark when I step into C's Pub. My eyes are slow to
adjust to the dim lighting. Scanning the large space, I spy
Owen in the back at one of the tables. We're meeting for an
early dinner before the corporate crowd flows in after work.

Sprawling down onto the chair across from him, I bump
the fist he holds out. "Hey, how's it going?"

"Things have been crazy. You can't even imagine."

If he only knew. "Oh, I think I can."

"I already ordered for you. I'm starving and didn't want to
wait around."

"Sounds good. Do you want to tell me what's got you so
worked up?"

"Yeah, but only Trevor knows about this and I don't want
it going any further than you two."

"That goes without saying, brother. What's up?"

"Eliza's pregnant... with twins." He blanches just telling
me. I bark out a laugh without meaning to, but the odds of

us going through this at the same time are slim. That being said, knowing he's in the same predicament makes me feel better.

"Dude, it's not funny. I'm wicked stressed. I'm trying to pretend everything's going to be great to reassure Eliza, but I'm completely overwhelmed."

"I wasn't laughing because I think it's funny. Well, in a way I do." He scowls and I hold up my hand. "Hear me out. It's a little amusing to me because I just found out at Thanksgiving that I'm going to be a father."

"What?" Owen is shocked.

"You heard right. I'm going to be a father to a baby girl in May."

"Holy shit. Are you freaking out? Who's the mother? Do you have a girlfriend I don't know about?"

"Her name is Tenley and she's my cousin Sophie's best friend."

"She lives in D.C.?"

"Yeah, which is why I've been going down there more."

"Are you guys together?"

"No, we're not a couple, but if I was ever going to settle down with someone, it would be her."

"Sounds like you don't have much choice now."

"I wouldn't say that. We're going to parent together, but we're not going to be in a relationship. She knows hockey is number one with me."

"She's okay with that?"

"She seems to be. Tenley isn't like most girls her age. She's mature and down to earth. If this had to happen with anyone, I'm glad it's her."

"If she's that great, maybe you guys will end up together."

"Maybe. It's too premature to know what's going to happen. The baby will be born and we have to work out a way for me to be involved as much as I can. Hopefully I'll get an offer from a team and that will alleviate any financial concerns. But there's so much up in the air still."

"Wow. I think you're handling this better than me."

"You're having twins. That's enough to scare the bejesus out of any guy."

"It does. And I feel bad because I want to be there for Eliza, but inside I'm a panicked mess."

"You're not having doubts about the two of you, are you?"

"No. Never. I wouldn't have asked her to marry me if I was. It's mostly about all the changes about to take place."

"When did she tell you?"

"The night I proposed. I asked her to marry me and when she mentioned we'd be having twins in seven months, I passed out."

I laugh uncontrollably. "Dude, that's hilarious. Where were you?"

"At your mother's shop. She never told you?"

"No, not a word. My mom's a great secret keeper. When is Eliza's due date?"

"Early June."

"Dude, we're going to be dads right around the same time. Tenley is due around mid-May. Our kids can grow up together. How cool is that?"

"That's awesome. I feel better knowing you're going through all the same stuff as me. Does that make me selfish?"

"No, it makes you human."

"Hey. How are you feeling?" I lie back on my bed with a relieved sigh. Practices have been brutal with coach cracking down on the entire team. He's been relentless.

"I'm good. I've been pretty energetic. I even hit the gym a couple of times this week."

"Is that safe for the baby?"

"Absolutely. I asked my doctor at my first visit. She said as long as I feel up to it and don't overdo it, everything will be fine."

"I feel like I haven't seen you in months, never mind three weeks. Are you showing more?"

She snorts. "Yeah. I definitely have a noticeable bump now."

"Oh God." I groan.

"What?"

"Please don't call it a baby bump."

"Why not?"

"Because it's fucking annoying. Whenever someone famous gets pregnant they always mention the person's baby bump and take pictures. It's the dumbest thing."

"I kind of like it."

"You can call it that all you want as long as you don't do it around me."

"What would you like me to call it?"

"Your stomach."

"That's boring. You have to do better than that."

"Mommy mound?"

She laughs. "Ugh. No."

"Hey, I kind of like that."

"You are not calling my stomach a mommy mound. It's too weird."

"I have the perfect solution. Why don't we just call it your stomach and be done with it?"

"Fine."

"How's everything else been? Anything got you worried?"

"If by anything you mean my mother, then no. I haven't spoken to them at all this week. It's been nice. I'm horrible for saying that."

"No, you're not. She shouldn't worry you. Parents are

supposed to make their kids feel better, not worse. We won't make that mistake with our little girl."

"How's hockey going? You haven't mentioned it the last few times we've spoken."

"I know. Coach has been kicking our asses."

"How come?"

"We have the Beanpot Tournament coming up next week."

"Is that a big deal?"

"You don't know what the Beanpot is?"

"I really don't."

"How does the mother of my child not know this?"

"Well, she would if you'd stop being dramatic and tell her," she teases.

"It's an annual hockey tournament between Boston University, Boston College, Northeastern, and Harvard. It's been taking place since nineteen fifty-two, so it's steeped in tradition. The Beanpot always takes place the first two Monday nights in February and it's become *the* battle for Boston's hockey bragging rights. The game is played at the TD Garden, which is fucking awesome. There's nothing like taking the ice in that arena. The crowds are wild and the cheering is louder than any other game I know of."

"It sounds like a big deal. Can I come watch?"

Her question is unexpected. Would I want her there watching me play? It would be nice for her to see what I work so hard for. Sometimes it seems like people have no idea how much work it is to train at this level. More than having her watch me skate is the desire to spend some time with her. I've missed her every single day we've been apart.

"Yeah, you can come. But would that be too much for you?"

"No. It's a short flight."

"Is it safe for you to fly with the baby?"

"Of course. Do you think I would suggest something that's not safe?"

"No, I know you wouldn't. Are you sure you want to come?" I don't want her to feel obligated to do something just to make me happy.

"Look, if you don't want me to visit, you need to tell me. This pregnancy has ruined my ability to read between the lines."

"Are you kidding? I can't wait to see you."

"Are you one hundred percent on board with this, because I look pregnant. Anyone who sees us together will know that I'm having your baby. If you want to keep it a secret I won't come. And I won't be angry about it."

"Just because I haven't told most of my friends yet, doesn't mean I don't want to. It's difficult to find the time where I can bring it up."

"I understand. It's not really locker room talk."

"Right. And if I tell a few and not the rest, it will get repeated and twisted about until rumor has it I impregnated an alien or some other sci-fi storyline."

She giggles. "I might look like a pregnant alien at this point."

"I bet you look beautiful."

"You'd be the only person to think so."

"Now I know you're lying."

She doesn't say anything and I know for whatever reason she's uncomfortable with me saying she's beautiful. She better get used to it. I plan to tell her many more times.

"I'm going to book my ticket when we hang up."

"How about you let me book it for you? I don't want you spending money you don't have to."

"I have some saved up."

"I'm sure you do, but let me get this for you. You're coming to watch my game." We've never really had the chance to discuss money, but I have a decently padded savings from my grandparents. I don't dip into it often.

"How does this work? You said it's the first two Mondays in February, so which one do I come for?"

"It's tough to pick. In a perfect world, we win the first week and play in the championship game the second week. But if we don't win our game, then we play the other team that lost in the consolation game. I'd like you to see me in the championship game and I'm going to be optimistic and buy your ticket for the second game. How many days can you be here for?"

"I have to meet up with some classmates on Saturday late-morning. I'd reschedule, but the project is due this week and we have to finish it. I can leave on Saturday afternoon after my classes are through and stay until Tuesday morning. If that's okay for you."

"Sure. Will you be okay staying at the frat house with me? I'll let you have my room. Or you can stay at my mom's house." Please stay with me. I want to spend every minute I can with her.

"I'd rather be with you. It would be weird to stay with your mom."

I smile in relief. "I'll book the flight and send you the information. I'm excited to see you." I hesitate. Oh, what the hell? "I've missed you."

I hear her long exhale and I wonder if she'll answer.

"I've missed you too."

The words settle warmly in my chest and I smile.

After we hang up, I look up flights and find one that leaves late afternoon like she needs. I text her the information and forward the confirmation email to her. I can't believe I'm going to see her in another week. Hopefully the time will pass quickly. I feel like a little kid waiting for Christmas to arrive.

CHAPTER EIGHTEEN

Tenley

THE FLIGHT IS SO QUICK IT BARELY FEELS LIKE WE'RE UP before we're heading in for the landing. Once I'm off the plane, I head toward our arranged meeting point. The walk to get there seems to be taking forever. The anticipation of seeing Clancy is making it feel longer than my flight.

I spot Clancy before he notices me. He stands head and shoulders above everyone else. And the scowl on his face every time someone comes too close to him is hilarious and has me grinning uncontrollably. I don't take my eyes off him, so I'm aware the moment he catches sight of me. His manly lips part, baring his straight, white teeth. His eyes sparkle with happiness and my stomach gets that fluttery feeling that only happens with him.

Before I realize it, my bag is on the ground and I'm in his arms. We stand there wrapped up in each other. Breathing in his masculine scent has my head spinning. I'm dizzy with longing, but I'm content at the same time. Cushioned against his chest with his arms sheltering me feels safe, and all my worries fade away. I want to remain here forever, or at least until I have the baby.

Clancy kisses the top of my head before he pulls away. Holding on to both my arms, he looks me over and smiles. "You look amazing. I can't even tell you're pregnant."

"Ha. You say that now, but that's because I have so many layers on." I glance down at my blue peacoat.

"Let's get out of here. I want to get you back to the house and feed you."

His home takes us thirty minutes to get to.

"It would usually be fifteen, but we got caught in some traffic. However, we're lucky it wasn't worse considering the time of day. We could've gotten caught up in all the commuters. Boston traffic on a bad day could give the Capital Beltway competition."

He pulls in to a wide driveway running beside the house and parks in front of the garage. My gaze curiously skims over the large, white house. "How many guys live here?"

"Ten, including me. We could actually fit one or two more, though." He gives me a look reminding me to stay in my seat and hurries around to help me out.

A cold breeze whips around us, sending a chill down my spine. I snuggle down inside my scarf. "Do you ever get sick of being around people all the time?"

"All the time." He winks, grabbing my bag from the back of the cab and slinging it over his shoulder.

"Come on." He holds out his hand and I slide mine into his hold. "Go slow on this brick walkway. I salted it earlier, so it would melt any ice, but it's still cold enough that it might not have helped."

Sliding my feet along, I do as he says, although I'm sure he'd never let me fall. His grip tightens as we climb the front stairs.

"Don't move," he cautions as he unlocks the door. He ushers me inside and I pause to gape at my surroundings. The foyer is huge and has a crystal chandelier hanging in the middle of the ceiling. I'm amazed it hasn't been shattered during one of their wild parties. There's a central hallway with rooms spilling off both sides and a staircase that Clancy points to. "My room is up here." He directs me to walk in front of him. When we reach the top, he says, "All the way to the end, last room on the left."

Stopping in front of his door, I glance at him. He jiggles his keys with a smirk. "I always lock my door. The savages I live with will take all my shit if I don't."

I'm not sure what I expected to find when I step inside, but it's not the neatly made bed and carefully organized space. This room looks like he put some effort into the decor. The navy blue and gray striped comforter matches the navy blue curtains flanking both windows. There's a large, gray area rug and an old, brown leather recliner in the corner. Pottery and books line the shelves above his desk and there's a tall bureau between the windows.

"What's wrong?" Clancy questions.

"Nothing at all."

"You seem surprised."

"I am. I guess I expected this room to have dirty laundry sprinkled about and naked pics of women on the walls."

He lets out a deep belly laugh. "Nah, that's not really my style. You haven't had a chance to see until now that I prefer things organized. Even the rest of the house stays pretty clean. The guys know it makes me crazy when it's not. And no one wants to deal with me when I get on a cleaning tear."

I giggle at the thought of him in an apron running around with a bottle of bleach.

"What?"

"I just had a funny image of you in my mind."

"Does it involve a feather duster and me using it on you?"

"No. But you did have an apron on."

"Hah. If anyone's going to be seen in a maid's uniform it will be you."

"I hate to break it to you, but I'm here for a hockey game, not to help you live out your freaky sex fantasies."

"Damn. Now you tell me." He grins shark-like before setting my bag down on his bed. "There's room in my closet if you want to hang anything up. I hate living out of a suitcase when I go away, so I cleaned out one of my bureau drawers for you too."

Wow, that was unexpected and so kind. "Thank you. I don't want you to go to any trouble for me." I'm here to visit and watch his tournament. Hopefully he didn't go out of his way too much. Being a bother is the last thing I want.

"Say no more." He waves a hand in dismissal of the topic. "I'm going to cook you some dinner. What do you think about that?"

"I'm not sure." Does he know how to cook? "If you're a good cook, then I'm happy. If this is the first meal you've made and I'm your test subject, then I'll pass."

He shakes his head. "I'm a great cook. I've got ribs slow cooking in the crockpot and I'm making baked potatoes with all the fixings. I've even got some veggies just for you."

"Yum, don't tease me. I'm starving."

"Why didn't you tell me? I would've grabbed you something on the way home."

"No, you don't understand. I'm in a permanent state of hunger no matter how much I eat."

"I guess it's a good thing I'm used to cooking for a dozen guys then."

"Mmm, who taught you to cook so well?" The ribs are practically melting in my mouth.

"My mom and my grandmother."

"No ex-girlfriend?"

"No." He chuckles. "Definitely not."

"Have you always been anti-relationship?"

"I never said anything about not being for relationships. I just haven't immersed myself into any because I've known since I was ten years old what I wanted to do with my life. Getting to the NHL is only the first part of my goal. A career in the NHL is a lot of work. I know there are plenty of players who are married and have kids, but I've always thought it would be better to avoid any complications."

Angling my head his way, I arch a brow. "How's that working out for you?"

"Up until that wedding last August, it was working out great." He flashes a quick grin.

"Yeah, that's the funny thing about making plans. The universe steps in and knocks your feet right out from under you and says 'what are you going to do now?'"

He shrugs. "There's not much you can do but grind away. We push through and find a way to make the most of the new plan. I don't regret being with you. I can never regret that night. First of all, it was phenomenal. Christ, I'm getting hard just thinking about it." He grimaces, adjusting himself through his jeans. "And now you're a human incubator for our baby girl. How can playing hockey compare with what you're doing?"

"It can't, but only because you're comparing apples and oranges. Making the NHL is not something many can boast about."

"I know, but my claim to fame is I'm a talented hockey player."

"Don't downplay your talent," I scold.

"It's still only a game, no matter how you look at it. Yes,

I'll be able to make an incredible living doing what I love, but it's not life altering on the level giving birth is."

The sound of the front door closing has us both pausing the conversation. It sounds like a train is rolling through the house and then a handful of guys pile into the kitchen at the same time.

"Damn. Something smells amazing."

"Get in my belly."

"Sure, I'll eat again."

"Hey, honey. We're home."

"Who is this gorgeous creature?" Tall, dark, and handsome saunters my way.

"Flynn, don't even think about it. She's the mother of my child."

"Oh." He freezes in place, eyes wide open, and all the comments stop. Flynn makes back up sounds as he moves away from us.

I laugh and look the other four guys over. No one seems surprised Clancy has a baby mother. I guess he shared the news with them and they took it well. There's no sign of surprise on their handsome faces.

Holy Hell. What's up with all these guys being so freaking hot? Is this some genetically superior frat? Is there some gene altering experiment going on here?

"Guys, you can come meet Tenley if you'd like."

"I'm Oliver. I play on the Terriers with Clancy. I don't live here. My girlfriend and I have an apartment."

The next one steps forward before I have a chance to answer.

"I'm Nolan. I'm a running back on the football team. It's nice to meet you."

I decide to wait until they're all done to say anything.

"Hey, I'm Donovan. I'm on the team with Clance."

"I'm Darren. I play football, and I've gotta know how Clancy got ahold of a babe like you."

"I'm Flynn. But you already knew that. I play football; the real man's sport." He lifts his chin at me with a cocky smirk.

"It's great to meet you all. It's overwhelming, but great."

"So, I hate to interrupt, but how much food is left over so we can eat?" Flynn questions. "You made enough to feed a small army."

"Or a small pregnant girl," Clancy winks at me.

"It's funny because it's true." I nod.

"No, really. What's up for grabs here, because I'm starving."

Clancy stands and pushes his chair back. "Let me borrow your plate for one minute." He holds his hand out and I pass it over. He moves to the counter and dishes more ribs from the crockpot onto my plate. He adds some more potatoes and green beans too. Returning, he sets it down in front of me. "I wanted to make sure you have enough before these scavengers pick at the rest."

"This should do nicely," I say, my fork already dipping in for more.

The guys grab plates and divvy up the rest of the dinner. At one point, Darren and Flynn almost come to blows over the last baked potato, but Clancy steps in, judiciously cutting it in half. I smile pridefully. He's going to make a great father.

———

"Are you tired?" Clancy questions as we watch the Bruins game.

"A little bit. I might doze off on you, but it's not because I don't want to stay awake. I've had a busy day."

"You're not feeling bad are you?" His eyebrows dip toward the middle of his forehead in concern.

"No, I feel fine. I'm just a little tired."

"I'm going to sleep in the recliner if that's okay with you."

"I feel bad taking your bed. Why don't you just sleep here with me? It's a huge bed and I don't move around much. Ever since spending freshman year sleeping on a twin sized mattress, it got me used to staying in one spot."

"I'll take the recliner. Do you know how many times I've slept all night in that? It's soft as butter and so comfortable."

"You know what I was thinking?"

"Nope."

"We need to come up with a name. It would be nice to be able to call her by her actual name instead of just saying Mommy and Daddy love you."

"You tell her Daddy loves her?" His head snaps in my direction on the pillow he's lying on. He's clearly surprised.

"Of course I do. Why wouldn't I?"

"I don't know. I'm not there with you every day, so it would be understandable if you just said Mommy."

"It wouldn't be what's best for her. It's not our daughter's fault that we're not a couple. She needs two parents to thrive."

He carefully studies me to the point where I become self conscious. "What?" I squirm.

"How did you get so wise? You don't act like any of the girls I know."

"That's not saying much." I roll my eyes.

"That's not true. I'm going to introduce you to Eliza, Owen's fiancée. They're having twins in June."

"You didn't tell me that."

"I just found out recently."

"Yikes, twins. I couldn't handle that."

"Yeah, it would be a lot. Eliza has a daughter too. She's three, I think."

"Oh hell no. Three kids at twenty-one?"

"Next time you panic, just think about them and be grateful we only have to parent one baby."

"For sure."

"All my friends have great girlfriends. Except Oliver. I don't care for his girl."

"Does he know that?"

"No, of course not."

"You don't tell him he could do better?"

"No. Guys aren't like that. We don't interfere. When they break up someday, I'll say, 'I knew she wouldn't last.'"

"How is it helpful after the fact? If you told him now he might listen and get away from her."

He turns on his side, facing me. "No, he wouldn't. You don't know how guys work at all do you?" His index finger taps the tip of my nose.

"Nope. Not at all. Which is why I'm single."

"Have you dated at all since the wedding?"

"No. I didn't before I found out I was pregnant, and obviously now that I am, I'm not going to hook up with anyone. That would be weird."

He looks relieved.

"Have you? Been with anyone since the wedding?" I'm not holding my breath for the reply I want. It's been six months since we had sex and I'm sure he's had plenty of offers.

"No, I haven't."

"Huh?"

"You heard me right."

"You haven't been with any other girls? Not even for a hand job or a blow job?"

"I haven't so much as kissed a girl since we were together."

"Why not?"

"There's no concrete reason why I didn't before I knew you were pregnant. I wasn't interested in anyone else. Once I found out about the baby, it felt wrong to mess around. Which is weird, right? We're not together in that sense, but I feel a loyalty toward you I've never experienced before." He props his head on his hand and stares down at me. "I can't really explain why. I only know you make me a better man."

His sweet confession brings me to the verge of tears. I close my eyes and turn to face Clancy. "Can I hug you?" I really want to be close to him after hearing that. No man has ever been so open with me before.

"Like you need to ask. My body is yours in any way you need," he teases predictably, but it doesn't detract from what he already said. I know making jokes is his form of self-preservation. And his sense of humor is one of my favorite things about him. The more time I spend with him, the longer the list grows. Pretty soon it will be scroll-length and I'll be so deeply in love, I'll never find my way back out.

CHAPTER NINETEEN

Clancy

Slowly stirring from slumber, I bury my nose in Tenley's hair. She smells so good. Need curls low in my stomach. My cock can't get any harder than it already is. Rocking it against her ass has me groaning. Fuck. I want her so badly.

My eyelids languidly raise and reality settles in. Shit. I back away from Tenley like she's on fire and roll over. Staring up at the ceiling, I groan and try to urge my cock back down with my hand, but it's not going anywhere.

Waking up with Tenley on my mind has become the norm. But having her here in my bed is torture. My cock is painfully hard and I'd sacrifice a toe or two for her to jerk me off right now. I want to come, and not from my own hand. Is that too much to hope for?

Groaning, I slip to the edge of the mattress and rise. I run a hand over my face. Shit. I didn't plan to fall asleep with Tenley. The last memory I have before I fell asleep was her asking me for a hug. I guess I enjoyed it too much.

Grabbing the remote, I shut off the TV that's still on from last night and make my way into my en suite bathroom. I close the door behind me and turn on the shower. Once the water's hot, I step inside and let the strong stream beat down on my chest.

It's difficult to think of Tenley in my bed and not want to join her. But if I go back in there it's not going to remain innocent. I want her too much. I can't even say *want* at this point. It's more of an uncontrollable need. Gripping my cock, I stroke my hand up and down the length and replay the night we were together.

"I'm going to make this a night you never forget." She grips me, guiding me to her entrance. Slowly sinking down onto me, warm and wet, she moans.

"Christ." She rolls her hips, riding me slowly. Dragging out my pleasure. My hands cup her perky tits, palming and plucking her nipples. I squeeze their fullness.

Watching her slide up and down my length in my memory has me mimicking the motion with my hand. It doesn't take long for me to finish, groaning out her name.

I spend the remainder of my shower soaping up and thinking about what's going to happen once the baby's here. Will we somehow end up together, or will Tenley want things to remain the way they've been? I don't like things being out of my control. I was raised to do what's needed to get the result you want. This is the first thing I can't make turn out in my favor.

"So I forgot to ask you last night, how did your friends take the news of our pregnancy?" As soon as Tenley asks the question, her fork spears more pancake and she eats another bite. She can really pack the food away. Despite what she said about looking pregnant, I wouldn't know if she hadn't pointed it out.

"They were all great about it. There was some ribbing

about not knowing how to wrap my shit, but as soon as they heard I wore a condom they shut up. I think a few of them were freaked the fuck out about it."

"We're not the only ones this has happened to."

"I told them it only takes a pinhole. Flynn said he's going to double wrap from now on." I snigger.

Tenley giggles. "I like your friends. They were really welcoming last night."

"Yeah, they're a cool bunch. I'm lucky we've been able to keep assholes out of the frat house, for the most part."

"You are. I've heard so many horror stories about sororities, I'd never want to deal with any of that."

"We never did come up with a name for the baby last night. Want to see what we can agree on?"

"Sure. Are there any family names you want to use?" she inquires.

"No, I want her to have her own name."

She puts her fork down and folds her hands on the table. "What about Sara?"

"Nah, I knew a Sara in elementary school who used to pick her nose."

Tenley rolls her eyes. "What about Caroline?"

"No, it makes me think of a Red Sox game."

"Huh? Clearly, I'm missing something."

"You know that song, right?"

"Yep."

"It's played at every Red Sox game before the bottom of the eighth inning."

"So we can't give that name to our daughter?"

"No, it will be weird."

"You're weird. It's a nice song. How many people can say there's a cool song with their name? I can't. No one even gets the spelling of my name right. Do you know how to spell it?" She raises an eyebrow in challenge.

"T.E.N.L.E.E." I grin.

"Are you serious?"

"I'm screwing with you. I know it's T.E.N.L.E.Y."

"You can contribute any name suggestions you have."

"What if I don't have any?" I'm not good at this stuff. I'd rather have her give me options.

"You don't like any female names?"

"I do, but I can't come up with any off the top of my head. Keep rattling off more and I'll bite on one sooner or later."

"Hmm, what about Mary, for the blessed mother?"

"Are you religious?" I don't even know this about her.

"No, I was kind of making a joke, but it was a bad one. I'm not against religion. I'd consider myself more spiritual than religious. I believe in a higher power, but I don't go to church, much to my parents' shame."

"Mary is a nice name and the sentiment that goes along with it is great, but it's kind of heavy for a little girl. I'd like something a little more modern or fun."

She gives me the stink eye. "You're being picky for a dude who hasn't given me even one option."

Racking my brain, I run through all the classmates' names I can remember. I dismiss each one as I remember, for one reason or another. "What about Molly?"

"Molly. Molly. Hmm." She props her chin on her fist. "Molly." She nods. "I like that. It sounds young and it's the name of some cute, little freckled face girl. Molly Wilde."

Whoa. Did she say Wilde?

"Wilde?" I whisper hoarsely.

"Yeah, don't you want her to have your last name?"

"Of course I do. I just assumed you'd want her to have yours."

"Maybe we can make mine her middle name?"

"I like that idea. Molly Davenport Wilde. It sounds great. And it's meaningful."

Her smile is wide as she places her palm on her stomach. "I love it. Molly Davenport Wilde, we love you."

The shrill sound of the whistle cuts the play short.

"Wake up. You guys are playing like you're half asleep," Coach shouts.

My eyes climb up the side of the arena seating, settling on Tenley. Her attention is fixed on what's going on down here. Does she like watching me practice? Is she impressed?

"Let's try that play again," Coach barks. "Wilde," he calls me over.

"Coach?"

"Is that your girl sitting up there?" He leans his head in the direction of Tenley.

"Yes, sir." I don't bother to correct him and say she's not my girl. That's a technicality and it wouldn't go over well right now. Coach is big on respect and I do my best to give him his due. He wants the best for us.

"You're playing well, but some of these guys could use a kick in the ass. The Beanpot is tomorrow. You might want to have words with them and wake them up."

"I will, coach."

He pats me on the back. "This is good practice for you. You'll be having many motivational talks with your child over the years to come."

"Yes, sir. I know I will."

"Get going," he dismisses me and I skate over to my teammates.

"Guys, we need to get our heads out of our asses. Coach just reminded me the Beanpot is tomorrow night. This is the championship game and we can have bragging rights for an entire year if we win. An entire year. We haven't won the

Beanpot in five years. Five fucking years. I don't know about you guys, but I don't want to hand over the cup to the Northeastern Huskies. They won it last year. They probably think they're going to win it again tomorrow night." I glance at Oliver. "What do you have to say about that?"

"No fucking way." He shakes his head.

"What about you, Donovan? You're new to the team this year, what do you think about the Huskies winning?"

"Hell no. We're going to crush them."

"You think? Because I think if we play the way we are right now, we're going to be embarrassed by them. Do you guys want to leave TD Garden tomorrow night with our heads hanging in shame?"

"No," they chorus.

"You're damn right we're not going to leave that way. This is our championship to win. How bad do you want it?"

"Bad," they shout.

"Then fucking show it. Get your shit together. Now let's play hockey."

"Yeah," they call out, raising their sticks in the air.

Coach blows his whistle. "Let's go."

"The second half of practice went much better. You guys need to remember those basic commandments that apply no matter what level you're playing at." Coach glances around the locker room to make sure everyone is listening. "Wilde, give me an example of something you need to remember for tomorrow's game."

"Never make blind passes. Do not pass the puck through the middle unless you're fucking sure it's in the clear."

He raises his thumb when I'm done. "There's one. Donovan, give me another."

"Make direct passes. Look where you're passing and send the puck forcefully."

Coach nods and raises his index finger. He points to Oliver.

"Plays need to be made quickly. When you hesitate, it gives your opponent time to figure out your play and break it up."

Another finger ticks off. "Shaw, give me one," he tells our goalie.

"The play is moving and you need to be too. Keep your head up, so you can read and react to the play."

Coach holds up four fingers. "Remember these four basic rules. They should be ingrained in your brains by now, but it's still good to remind yourself. Now get out of here. And when I see you tomorrow, I want everyone well rested and ready to win the Beanpot." He walks from the locker room.

"Do you think we have a chance of winning this thing?" Donovan questions, a frown creasing his brow.

"Of course. We have just as much chance as they do," I reply.

"They beat us in our last game, but it was early in our season. We have their number now. We just need to play our game and put them on their heels," Oliver jumps in.

"Guys, we all have jobs to do tomorrow night and we're going to fucking do them. That's all there is to it. Now get out of here and forget about the Beanpot until tomorrow. That doesn't mean it's okay to go out and get shitfaced. No drinking tonight, fellas." It's only one night of the year."

"Are you and Tenley going out?" Oliver asks.

"No. We're heading back to the house. She has to be tired by now, and I want to hang out with her."

"I'll see you tomorrow." Oliver holds out his fist.

Bumping it with my own, I reply, "Get ready to battle, brother."

CHAPTER TWENTY

Tenley

"I WAS GOING TO TAKE YOU STRAIGHT HOME BUT SOME OF my friends are out and they want to meet you. Are you up for it?"

"Of course. Do me a favor and turn the heat up. I'm frozen solid."

"You shouldn't have sat there for so long. I'm sorry. I don't know why I didn't think of bringing a blanket for you."

"I'm fine. It wasn't until we got outside that I caught a chill. The rink wasn't even cold."

"How did you like watching?" His eyes flick in my direction before returning to the road. Is he worried that I didn't enjoy it?

"I loved it. You're really good."

He smiles. "You don't have to say that. I know not everyone loves hockey like I do."

"I like hockey, but I don't know much about it."

"I can teach you. Actually, you and Molly can learn together."

I smile at his use of her name. "I'm really in love with that name now. I'm glad we chose it."

"Me too." He signals to pull over and parks next to the curb. "I got you as close to the pub as I can."

"Stop worrying about me. I'll be fine."

"That's not going to happen."

We hurry toward the pub. Clancy's arm is around me, sheltering me from the cold. The interior of C's is dark and loud. I can barely see where he's leading me, but he's as sure-footed as ever. He pauses next to a table with two other couples.

"Hey," the four of them call out.

Clancy's hand is comforting in the middle of my back. Meeting his friends is intimidating.

"This is Tenley. She's a junior at King University."

"I'm Eliza. It's great to meet you."

"Hi. I've heard a lot about you." My eyes dip to her noticeable bump.

"This is Owen," Eliza pats the chest of the large guy next to her. Damn, another hot friend of Clancy's.

"How are you doing, Tenley?" His voice is deep.

"I'm great thanks."

"I'm Trevor and this is Grace," the other gorgeous guy at the table speaks.

"Hi. I'm glad to meet you both."

"Have a seat." Clancy pulls out a chair for me, settling in the one at the end of the table.

"You guys don't play hockey, but you look like athletes." They're large guys and obviously in shape. "Hmm, are you football players?"

"Yep." Owen nods. "I'm the quarterback and Trevor is a wide receiver."

"Although, our season has been over for a couple of months now," Trevor explains.

"Are you all students at B.U.?"

Grace nods. "We are. We're all seniors, like Clancy."

"How are you feeling?" Eliza asks.

"I've been doing really well. The second trimester has been relatively easy. I'm waiting for the fatigue to hit me again, though."

"You may be fine the rest of the way. Everyone is different."

"How are you doing? Is it easier this time because you've been through it before? Or is it the opposite?"

"I think it's a little easier because I know what to expect and what I can and can't eat or do. But I'm having twins this time and I'm showing much faster."

"Two buns in the oven, Eliza. There's no mystery why that's happening," Clancy teases.

"It's not like I can forget that." She rolls her eyes.

"Can we just talk about the elephant in the room?" Trevor holds his palms up. "How did you get the 'Wilde Man' off the market?"

"I didn't." Is he technically off the market? We're not together. He hasn't been sleeping with anyone else, but that will probably end once the baby is born.

"Girls at Boston University will be crying themselves to sleep every night."

"Shut it, dude." Clancy raises his middle finger.

"I can't wrap my head around it. You're the least likely person I know to be tied down, and now you're going to be."

Clancy shrugs. "It is what it is. I want to be a part of my daughter's life."

Does that mean he's putting up with me because he has to if he wants to be involved? I hope not.

"Trevor, don't be insensitive," Grace scolds.

"Hey, I'm not trying to be. I'm just talking to my boy."

"Hi, Clancy." A beautiful blonde stops next to him. "Haven't seen you around lately. What's keeping you so busy?" She twirls her hair around her finger.

Is she thrusting her boobs in his face or is it me? Yeah, she definitely is.

"Same old. Hockey and school take up all my time."

He's not rushing to tell her I'm his baby momma.

"Well, sounds like you're overdue for some fun. Give me a call and I can help you with that."

I bet she'd like to help with a lot of things.

"Sounds good."

Sounds good? Is this the kind of girl he's attracted to? If it is, then what's he doing with me?

"I'll be in touch." She wiggles her fingers in a wave and shakes her ass to the other side of the bar.

I roll my eyes and Eliza sniggers. Busted. Oh well. I'm sure she understands my disgust. What woman wouldn't?

"Your friends seem nice. I really like Eliza and Grace."

"I'm glad you made plans with Eliza for tomorrow. I have class anyway. You might as well have something to do."

"We can talk about pregnancy issues. It's nice to know someone else my age who's going through it at the same time."

"I feel like that, too, with Owen."

Burrowing down into the covers, I shiver. Clancy notices.

"Come here. Let me warm you up." He draws me back against him until my back is pressed to his chest.

"You're so hot."

"So I've been told."

"Listen, egomaniac, I'm talking body temperature, not looks."

"If you say so."

"You're impossible." My eyes drift closed. Cuddled against him, I'm so relaxed. He shifts behind me and I feel something pressing into my ass. A very large, hard thing is poking into me. Adjusting my position, I brush against him and he moves backward. Doesn't he want me? I want him so badly I'm crazed with desire. I scoot toward him until we're in contact once more.

"Tenley," he grits out.

I roll over until I can see his face. "What?"

"You know what. You're playing with fire."

"Maybe I want to get burned."

"You don't mean that."

"Don't dismiss what I say. If you don't want me that's fine. But don't act like you're doing me a favor."

"I never said I didn't want you. But I care enough about you that I don't want you to have any regrets."

"The only regret I'm going to have is if I leave without having an orgasm by your hand... or mouth... or..."

He crashes his lips into mine, silencing me. His tongue commandingly sweeps into my mouth, seeking out mine. Dancing together, each stroke and thrust is matched. Kissing him after all this time is as electric and natural as I remembered. He moves between my legs pressing his hard cock against my clit and a breathy moan escapes into his mouth. I'm so wound up, I'm already on the verge of coming.

Clancy's hand slips inside my pajama bottoms.

"Christ, you're so wet." He drags my juices over my clit, slowly drawing circles as if we have all the time in the world.

"Oh God, that's so amazing. Don't stop."

"No way," he rumbles against my neck before his lips skim over the delicate area beneath my ear. His teeth nibble on my lobe before his tongue soothes the sting away.

His fingers move faster, flicking and rubbing the engorged bundle of nerves and my hips rock as I seek my release. Gripping his hair, I tug his lips to mine just before I unravel with my orgasm.

He swallows my cries of pleasure, exhaling his own when my hand slides into the shorts he's wearing.

"Oh, fuck. Your hand feels fucking amazing."

"Get on your back," I order and he complies. I tug on both sides of his shorts and he raises his hips to help me. I draw them down his legs and throw them to the floor without taking my eyes off his rigid cock. Watching as my fingers close around him feels like an out of body experience. I've wanted this for so long... since the night we were together. I've been afraid to admit that to myself, but it's true. There hasn't been a day that's passed where I haven't thought about what touching him felt like or how having him inside me fills me up.

Stroking from the base to the tip, I reacquaint myself with the soft texture of his skin. Lowering between his legs, I lick the tip, collecting the bead of moisture on my tongue.

"Don't tease me," he growls, and I slide my lips down over the head, taking him all the way in. His hands go to my head, urging me to climb up and lower down. I let him control the pace and he has me moving increasingly faster until he's fucking my mouth. I love the forceful way he's holding my head and using my mouth. Urgent and animalistic, his hips thrust, repeatedly triggering my gag reflex until he comes with a harsh groan. He shudders through his release, holding me down on his cock. I swallow down his come, letting my tongue trail up the length until I release him. Pleasing him is exciting and satisfying.

He runs a shaky hand over his brow. "Holy shit. That was fucking intense." I beam pridefully, pleased with myself.

Catching me around my waist, he flips me to my back and tugs my bottoms off before I realize it. "You're so gorgeous. All those curves..." His eyes close for a brief moment. "I need to see if you taste as good as I remember."

Lowering to his stomach, he raises my legs over his shoulders, fingers gripping the outside of my thighs. He swipes his tongue along the length of my slit. "Mm, just like I remember." He plucks my clit between his lips, sucking gently and flicking it with his tongue until I can't control my hips. They move of their own accord, rocking and rubbing against his mouth until I explode, releasing so intensely every inch of me is quivering.

He raises his head and grins. "That was fun. Why have we waited this long to do that?"

"I'm not sure," I gasp, still out of breath. "But I don't want to wait so long before we do it again."

"No chance of that happening. You just reminded me of what I'm missing out on."

"Should we...?" I arch an eyebrow.

"Fuck?" he asks.

"Yeah."

"Not tonight. Let's see how we feel tomorrow. I don't want to rush you into anything. And I don't want you to feel obligated to have sex with me just because we have in the past."

"That's not why. Sex with you was hot. I want to see if it's still as good." I already know it is. Really I just want to be that close with him.

"Judging from what just happened, I'd say it's even hotter than it was before."

"We might have to do that again, so I can make sure."

"I think you're right."

CHAPTER TWENTY-ONE

Tenley

"THANKS SO MUCH FOR MEETING ME THIS MORNING." I smile at Eliza.

"Oh please." She waves her hand. "You just saved me from turning cranky. I'm starving."

"I can't even imagine how difficult it must be to have two babies to feed."

"It's not that much different. But I feel huge already and I'm only five months."

"I've been lucky. I really only started to show about a week ago. My stomach popped out suddenly. I went to sleep one way and woke up another. It was kind of freaky."

"That's what happens."

My fingers play with the edge of the paper napkin under my glass. I have a million questions I want to ask her, but we only met last night. Will it be weird if I do?"

"Clancy was telling me you live in an apartment with some friends, but will probably move back home with your parents. Is that what you'll do?"

"Yeah, it's looking that way. I don't see how I'll be able to work with a newborn, unless I want to put her in daycare, which I don't."

"That's why family is so important. No one can do it all on their own."

"What about you guys? What are your plans?"

"It really depends what happens in the draft. We don't know where we'll end up."

"Wherever he goes, you go, right?"

"Definitely. I'm hoping it will at least be on the east coast. I really don't want to be all the way across the country. My family is all here."

"I can understand that. Maybe it's a blessing that Clancy and I aren't together. He'll move to whatever state he needs to and I'll stay in Virginia. He'll be the one doing all the travel to see Molly."

"Molly? You guys chose a name already?" Eliza smiles.

"Yeah. I really wanted to be able to call her by her own name. Have you guys picked yours yet?"

"No. We have the sonogram next week and then we'll get to it." Eliza raises her glass of water, taking a sip before she continues. "I feel like you have concerns and you're afraid to voice them."

"Maybe."

"Let them out, girl. Dwelling on things that worry you isn't good for you or the baby."

"Clancy's your friend and I don't want to put you in an uncomfortable position."

"Please." She rolls her eyes. "You're not. None of what you say will leave this table."

"I'm worried what will happen once the baby is born. He's going to get picked up by a team and move away. He'll be busy training and getting settled in. How's he going to have time to visit Molly?"

"And you?" Her observation is astute.

"Yes, and me. But I don't know why I feel that way. I don't want to. We're not a couple and I've never hinted I'd even like to be."

"But?"

"But, he's so sweet with me and we have a connection I've never shared with anyone else."

"And you want more?"

"I'm not sure." I grimace. "Okay, I do, but I'm scared. He's going to have women throwing themselves at him and I'll be the anchor weighing him down."

"In the time I've known Clancy, he's never been the type to do anything unless he wants to. If he chooses to be with you, then you don't have anything to worry about."

"He hasn't said anything to indicate he's interested in more than friendship. He might not feel the same as I do."

"Why don't you ask him?"

I shake my head vigorously. "I can't. It feels a little like begging to me."

"By asking him? How is that begging?"

"Not begging. Maybe pressuring? If we end up together, I want to know it's his choice."

"I understand that, but what if he's thinking the same way you are? If that's the case, you guys will both be settling for friendship when there could be more."

"You're right. Maybe I'll talk with him tonight when we get back to his place after the game."

"That's a great idea. What's the worst that could happen? You find out that you guys will only be friends? At least you'll know and can focus on your future."

I'm going to be brave enough to have this conversation with him tonight. I'm carrying his child and I need to know one way or another what my future looks like.

"Mom, this is Tenley. She's visiting from D.C.."

Mrs. Wilde steps forward. "I need to give the mother of my granddaughter a hug."

I smile and step into her. She soothingly rubs my back and tears sting my eyes. I wish my own mother would be warm and loving like this, instead of telling me what I should and shouldn't do. Blinking repeatedly, I hold the tears at bay. God I hate hormones.

"It's nice to meet you, Mrs. Wilde. I've heard great things about you."

"Please, call me Heidi. And the things you've heard are all true," she quips.

"I hate to rush off, but I need to get ready. I'll see you guys on the other side of the game." Clancy winks confidently.

"Good luck," I encourage.

"Come on. You can do better than that. No good luck kiss?"

Does he really want me to kiss him in front of his mother?

He nods, his full lips twisted into a smirk as if he can hear my thoughts. Raising my face, I purse my lips for an innocent peck. He wraps me in his arms and lowers his head slowly, drawing out the tension.

By the time our lips connect, I've forgotten his mother is standing there. I've forgotten everything but the sensation of his lips and the caress of his tongue tangling with mine. Fingers clutching his broad shoulders, I urge him closer. He draws back his tongue, slicking over his bottom lip as if he's savoring our kiss. His eyes are heated with desire, telling me we'll be continuing this later tonight. My knees feel weak as I back away.

"Good luck, dear." Heidi breaks through my hormone laden bubble and my cheeks flush with embarrassment.

Clancy walks away and Heidi smiles. "Why don't we find a

bathroom for you and then our seats. We can avoid the rush of the crowd."

"Smart thinking."

Seeing a hockey game live is completely different than watching it on television. Everything happens at a faster pace and I can barely keep up. Eyes snapping around the ice, I watch Clancy foil the Huskies' attempt at scoring. The crowd goes wild and I feel surprisingly proud.

Heidi leans toward me. "You know, I've never seen him so solicitous toward a girl. I can tell he really cares about you."

"He's a responsible guy. I'm carrying his daughter." I shrug.

"It's more than that," she offers, and my level of hope climbs. Is she right?

The group of girls on my other side catch my attention with their conversation. "Clancy is just as hot in bed as they say."

I can't see which one said this, but they're all attractive girls.

"When did you hook up with him?"

"Early August. We were both at C's and I went back to the frat with him."

"It was just the one time?"

"Yeah, but I'm hoping for a repeat tonight if they win." They all giggle and I force my eyes back to the game.

Clancy is racing around the ice, making plays left and right, but it's all a blur because I can't stop my mind from whirling with a tornado of questions.

Did he lie about sleeping with anyone else? Maybe he had sex with her after me.

Is this the way it's always going to be? Someone coming

out of the woodwork who's slept with him and wants a repeat?

I don't want to deal with rabid females looking to hook up with him every day of the week. I'll turn into a jealous shrew and that's not who I want to be. I've never been the jealous type, until now. My stomach is nauseous from the thought of his hands on her naked body and hers on him. I'd rather be alone than have him be mine for a period of time and then cheat on me.

Heidi grabs my arm as Clancy passes the puck to Donovan. He races down the ice and my gaze skips to the clock - five seconds remaining. Donovan approaches the net, sweeping the puck perfectly between the goalie and the right side of the net, scoring the game winning goal.

The Terriers players go wild along with the crowd.

Heidi and I hug, bouncing on our seats. I'm thrilled all their hard work has paid off. Clancy deserves this win. But I can't help but feel this win will put more distance between us, and in more ways than one.

The frat house is rocking with celebration when we arrive. Packed with bodies, I'm tempted to turn tail and run. Clancy must sense my hesitation. He grips my hand tighter and leads me to the kitchen where his friends are situated around the table.

Eliza rises, hugging me and I say hello to everyone I've met since coming to Boston. Owen gives up his chair for me and Eliza tugs on my arm, pulling me down into the seat next to her.

"Hey, great game." Her eyes sparkle with excitement.

"It really was," I reply. At least the parts I was paying attention to were.

Clancy is swallowed up by the crowd as they all congratulate him. I take in all the girls clamoring for his attention and it only saddens me more.

I slip my coat off and hang it on the back of the chair. My hand goes protectively to my stomach as I rub circles over the small mound.

"Is she kicking?" Eliza asks.

"Not right now. She's restless, though." Could she be reacting to my stress? I don't want to negatively impact her and if being in this atmosphere is doing so, then I need to remove myself from it.

Turning my head, I find Clancy hugging an attractive girl. Her toned body is encased in painted on jeans and a tight, low-cut shirt. He releases her but stays close, as if he doesn't want to be far from her. My chest pains when he smiles down at her upturned face.

I spin forward not wanting to see any more. Eyes closing, I breathe through my nose and try to calm myself. This changes nothing. Clancy and I weren't a couple and he never made any promises to me.

Eliza's hand on my arm has my eyelids snapping open. "Are you feeling okay?"

"I'm a little nauseous and tired. I think I'm going to head up to bed." Rising, I grab my coat, hanging it over my arm. "It was great seeing you again. Good luck with everything."

"You sound like we won't be seeing each other again."

"Just in case, it's been great getting to know you." Eliza looks concerned but only nods.

Spotting Clancy in the crowd is easy. He's taller than all of the girls and most of the guys. Edging through people, I keep a hand over my stomach and touch him on the arm.

"Tenley." He looks surprised.

Yeah, asshole, remember me?

"I'm gonna head up to bed. Can you unlock the door for me?"

He frowns. "Are you okay?"

"Yeah, just tired."

He takes my hand and leads me to the stairs. We plod up them side by side and when we're outside his room he turns to me.

"Are you sure nothing's wrong?"

"Yeah, what could be wrong?"

I love watching hot chicks fall all over the guy I'm in love with. Oh shit. Am I in love with him?

Gaze skating up his thick chest, I meet his hazel orbs and my stomach feels like a water spout is spinning wildly inside. Fuck me. I'm totally in love with him.

He opens the door for me and I slip inside, immediately heading to the bathroom. When I come out, he's sitting on the edge of the bed with his elbows on his knees. He stands and walks toward me.

Oh shit.

He stops when the toes of his sneakers almost touch mine. "What's really going on with you?"

"I'm tired. I think all the walking around and climbing the stairs at the arena wore me out."

"Are you sure that's all it is?"

I force myself to smile. "Yeah. Go back to your party."

"I'm fine with staying here with you."

But I'm not. If he stays he'll see me upset and I can't have that.

"No, really, I'm okay. I'll feel worse if you miss out on your celebration. You guys were awesome and you deserve to let off some steam."

"Did you think I was awesome?" He grins tugging me into his arms.

Lifting my face toward his, I nod sincerely. "I did. You were amazing."

His arms close, bringing me tight against the front of him. Turning my head, I press my cheek to his chest. Is this the last time he'll hold me like this? And then I imagine I can smell the perfume of the last girl he hugged and break free from his hold.

"I'm going to get in bed. I'll see you in the morning."

He studies my expression carefully before ticking his head in an unhurried nod. "If you need anything at all you text or come and get me."

"I will."

"I mean it. You're not going to interrupt anything that can't be interrupted. I'm only hanging out with some friends."

Is that what they call it?

"I know."

He steps backward and points. "Get some rest. I'll be back to check on you."

Once he's gone, I breathe a sigh of relief and change into a t-shirt and sleep shorts. I turn the lamp off and slip between his sheets. Snuggling into the pillow he slept on last night, I breathe in his scent. This is probably the last thing I need to be doing, but I'm a glutton for punishment. I should be doing everything I can to keep my mind off Clancy and here I am practically humping his pillow. When I get back home, I need to treat it as a fresh start. No more romanticizing things between Clancy and myself.

CHAPTER TWENTY-TWO

Clancy

GLANCING AT MY WATCH, I NOTICE THE LATE HOUR. FUCK me, this party keeps dragging on. All I want to do is go to bed. I've wasted four hours that could've been spent with Tenley, but instead, I'm fending off unwanted advances and doing my best to smile through them. I've been hugged and had my biceps caressed more than I want to think about. I know we won the game, but I wasn't the only one playing.

Flynn ushers the final partygoers out the front door. Everywhere I look there are empty red cups and beer bottles. Brushing my hair back from my face, I sigh.

"Dude, I got this. Go be with your girl."

"Really?" Flynn isn't known for chipping in on the clean up, or much else.

"Yep, I'll do it. How many times have you taken care of it for me?"

"Thanks, man. I didn't think you'd noticed."

Flynn raises his finger to his lips. "Shhh. Don't tell anyone. It's all part of my act."

I bark out a laugh and wonder how I didn't figure out his

game on my own as I climb the stairs. The lights are out inside my room and I can see Tenley under the covers.

I head to the bathroom and brush my teeth. I strip down to my underwear and t-shirt and slide in next to her. Lying on my back I replay everything that happened when she came up to my room. She seemed upset, but I can't imagine why. She was talking to Eliza at the table and I know she wouldn't upset Tenley.

Rolling over to my side, I wrap my arm around her. I don't want her to leave. I've enjoyed having her here. Once she's gone, I'm going to miss her. And I don't know when I'll be able to get down to D.C. again. I'm taking a full course load and it's my final semester. I can't afford to fuck it up. I want my degree before I head off to play professional hockey.

Lowering my face, I press my nose into her hair and inhale the scent of her floral shampoo. Instantly, it relaxes me. My eyes drift shut and I pretend Tenley is mine. I fall asleep with a smile on my face.

Rolling to my back, I groan. Every part of my body is sore from last night. We played a fucking hard game, battling to the end. My eyelids struggle to open and when they do, I realize I'm in bed alone. I sit upright and snap my head from one side to the other in search of Tenley. Did she leave? She wouldn't leave without saying goodbye, would she?

Jumping out of bed, I pull on last night's jeans and rake my fingers through my thick hair before tugging on a backwards ball cap.

I pad down the stairs on bare feet and hurry across the freezing cold hardwood floors. As I approach the kitchen I hear my friends laughing and smell bacon cooking. It's pretty early for them to be up after a game and a party. I have a pretty good idea of what the draw to be awake is, and it's not the bacon. Although bacon is enough to get me out of bed. Stepping into the kitchen, my suspicions are confirmed.

Tenley is cooking for the guys. Flynn stands next to her, whisking eggs in a glass bowl. The same Flynn who can't boil water without instruction.

Leaning against the door jamb, I observe the happenings.

"Then this other time Clancy got locked out of the house completely bare assed. The girl he messed around with stole his clothes and threw them in the neighbor's koi pond," Darren shares.

I'm half pissed off and half amused. Guess which one is winning out. "That's enough, Darren." I step forward into the space. Every set of eyeballs in the room goes wide. "What's the matter? Didn't think I'd hear?"

No one answers. Not that I expected them to. They know I'm an easygoing guy, but they can tell when I'm done playing and I mean business.

"Good morning," Tenley murmurs as she uses tongs to remove bacon from the pan. I edge in between her and Flynn and send him on his way with a fierce scowl. Flynn puts both hands up in front of his chest, backing away.

Picking up the bowl from the counter, I whisk the eggs some more. "What can I do to help you out?"

"Nothing. Go sit down with your friends. This is my thank you for letting me stay here."

"You don't need to thank me or pay me back in any way. I love having you here."

"Well, I still want to do it. And this is my only chance."

"Why is it your only chance?"

"I'm leaving in a little bit and I doubt I'll be back here before you find out which team will be snatching you up."

"Why won't you?"

"I won't be able to fly in another two months."

"You can come before then."

"Clancy, I have school."

"What about spring break?"

"I have things to do during that time."

"Like what?"

"Like painting the nursery and getting it set up. My mom mentioned having a baby shower then."

"Can I come down for that?"

"You want to come to the shower?"

"Sure."

"You do realize that most showers are girls only."

"No, I don't know anything about showers. But isn't that kind of sexist?" I jest.

"It's the way it's always been."

"I think we should shake things up and have a co-ed baby shower."

"Nope, not happening."

She peers over her shoulder as if she forgot there were other people sitting there listening to us. "Sorry guys. I forgot you were there."

"Ouch," Flynn comments. "You might be the first girl who's ever forgotten me."

"There's a first time for everything, dude." Oliver smirks.

"Did you stay over last night?" I ask.

"Yeah. I had a little too much to drink."

Now that I think of it, I didn't see his girlfriend at the game or party. Things might be on a downward slide with them.

Tenley plates the bacon and eggs for the guys and I help her pass them out. I fill a plate for her and direct her to the last open chair at the table.

"But what about you?" she asks.

"I'm not carrying a baby. I'll be fine."

Not a peep is heard from any of them as they inhale the delicious breakfast Tenley prepared. These fuckers need to find their own girls. She should still be in bed with me, all alone, so we could say a proper goodbye. I'm more than a little resentful that I'm sharing our last minutes together with all my housemates.

───────

I catch hold of her arm and step off to the side. "I can't go any farther than this without a ticket."

"Oh, yeah." She looks sad.

"Go right to your gate. I'm going to worry about you."

"I'll be fine. I'm a big girl. I'm about to be a mother."

"I know you are, but that doesn't mean I won't still worry."

"Thank you for everything. I had a great time."

"Are you sure? You've been off since last night and I can't figure out why."

"Stop worrying. You'll be relieved I'm gone. You can get back to life as you know it."

"Life as I know it is about Molly and you."

"You have a lot more to your life than us. Make the most of it. This is your last year of college."

What is she saying? Does she want me to have fun and party? I'm confused.

"Will you call me when you get home?"

"I will."

Stepping forward, I pull her into my embrace and try not to think about how this is the last time I'll hold her indefinitely. We have no concrete date scheduled to see each other.

"God, I'm going to miss you." My hands stroke up and down her spine.

"I'll miss you too."

Tipping her chin up with my fingers, I lower my head, capturing her lips with mine. Our kiss is a tender goodbye. I don't want to let her go, but we both have obligations we need to see through.

Brushing one more kiss over her lips, I straighten up. "Don't forget to call me. I'll be waiting to hear from you."

"I know. Now let me go before I miss my flight."

"I'm good with that. Then I could keep you." I wink.

"Bye for now." She presses her lips together in a small semblance of a smile.

"Talk soon." I wave.

She turns and walks away. I can barely restrain myself from running after her or calling out her name. *Don't leave. I never want you to go.* My stomach churns with worry. Something's off with her and she won't tell me what. Did she decide she doesn't want me involved in Molly's life? Because if that's the case, she'll have a fight on her hands. But I can't believe she'd do that until I hear the words from her lips. That can't be it. But what could be wrong?

I watch the clock like a hawk about to swoop in on its prey. My phone finally dings with a text, not a call.

Tenley: *I'm home. Great flight. All is well.*

Me: *Glad to hear it. Thank you for letting me know.*

Why did she text me instead of calling? Is she busy, or is there more to it? Or am I turning into a paranoid freak? At this point I don't know what to make of anything.

Me: *When will I talk to you again?*

Tenley: *Tomorrow?*

Why does she want to wait until tomorrow? There are still eight hours left today.

Me: *Why not tonight?*

Tenley: *I have a lot to do. Not sure I'll have time.*

If she needs tonight to get settled back in and catch up with her roommates, I can give her that time. I'll miss her. I already do, but there's nothing I can do about it. I can't force her to call me and I don't want to be a pain in the ass.

Me: *Okay. Talk tomorrow.*

"What's up with you?" I reach over and whack Oliver with the back of my hand. We're in our economics classroom waiting for the professor to arrive.

"I don't want to talk about it."

"Dude, get it off your chest. You'll feel better."

"Stacey's cheating on me."

"What?" I can't have heard him right.

"I walked in on Stacey with another guy."

"In your apartment?"

"Yep."

"What did you do?"

"I kicked his ass."

"What did she do?"

"She told me she wants me to move out."

"Oh fuck. Where will you go?"

"I don't know. I'll have to find someone looking for a roommate, I guess."

"We have space at the frat if you want in. It's not a great room, but it's better than being on the street or having some shit roommate."

"I'll take it. Then I can move my shit out immediately."

"What about all the furniture you have?"

"She can have it all. I just want my clothes and a few other things."

"When do you want to get your stuff? We can throw it in my truck and be done."

"How about this afternoon?"

"Works for me."

"How did it go getting Tenley to the airport yesterday?"

"She left." I shrug.

"Did you think she'd stay?"

"No, but I thought she'd be more torn up about leaving."

"You wanted her to cry?"

"Yes. No. I didn't want her to, but I expected her to. Her hormones are all screwed up and she cries easily. I don't know why she wasn't upset about leaving."

"Maybe she's okay because she knows you guys are friends."

"Yeah, but we were heading toward more than friends."

"Does she know that?"

"We fooled around the other night and that's not Tenley's style."

"Didn't you knock her up on a one-night stand?"

"Yeah, but I was the exception."

"Or so you think." He chuckles. "Maybe she tells all the guys that."

"Don't make me punch you in the face. You don't know Tenley like I do. I've known her for years and she's a nice girl. She's a relationship type of girl."

"Then why didn't she push for more with you?"

He makes a valid point. After the night we messed around, I expected things to be different between us; in a good way. I thought we'd talk about dating and see what happened.

"I have no idea. One minute everything was fine and the next she was acting strange."

"In my experience there's only one thing that makes girls act like that."

"What is it? Don't keep me waiting."

"The green eyed monster."

"Jealousy? You think?"

"I know. Women are territorial, and if someone comes on

to their man it causes problems even if the guy isn't to blame."

"I'm not saying you're right, but you could be. There were a lot of girls there that night. But I was mostly with the guys."

"You won't know unless you ask."

"I'll talk to her later and see what she says." Hopefully, I can get to the root of the problem.

CHAPTER TWENTY-THREE

Tenley

"I FEEL LIKE I HAVEN'T SEEN YOU IN AGES AND WE LIVE together," Cassie complains, sinking down at the table across from me.

"I've been back home for almost a week now. Where have you been?"

"I've been getting extra help with two of my classes."

"And that's taking up all your time?" I aim a skeptical look her way.

"Yep, most of it. That and studying."

"Why the sudden push to get better grades? What, is there a cute guy involved?" Cassie looks away. "Oh, I should've known this was about a hot guy. Nothing motivates you like that does."

"Shut up. I'm not that bad."

"Yeah, you are. At the least you could admit it. There's nothing to be ashamed about. We've all fallen for a handsome face."

"And a great ass," she retorts.

"Asses are okay, but I'm more of a shoulders and arms girl."

"And Clancy has those in spades."

I frown. He has a lot of good things, but I'm not supposed to be thinking about that.

"What's wrong? Is there trouble in paradise?" She leans forward on the table.

"We were never in paradise. And there's no real trouble. It's more like foreseeable trouble in my future."

"What the hell does that even mean?"

"He has girls throwing themselves at him all the time. I can't deal with the worry."

"Worry about what? That he'll cheat?"

"Yeah. How long can a guy resist that kind of temptation before he jumps? If women are always offering it up to him, sooner or later he's going to bite."

"Says you."

"Statistics say, not me."

"Well, you guys are more than a statistic and you should give him some credit. What has he done to make you think he's not trustworthy?"

"I saw him hugging some girl."

"Oh my God, a hug," she shrieks, rolling her eyes.

"It looked like more than a regular hug."

"Was she attractive?"

"Yes. And she had a flat stomach, unlike me."

"I get it. You feel unattractive. You're forgetting she's not carrying his baby. What makes you think he'd want anyone else?"

"He's a man."

"Don't be a man hater or a man doubter. No one likes those kind of people."

"I don't want to be like that, but it looked like he was enjoying hugging her and talking to her. It made me feel jealous because I want to be the only one he hugs and smiles at."

"You know that's not realistic or healthy, right?"

"If you say so."

"Tenley," she warns.

"I know. I think these hormones are making me go crazy."

"Why don't you ask him flat out who she was?"

"I can't do that."

"Why not?"

"It makes me sound terribly jealous."

"But you are exactly that."

"I know, but he doesn't need to be made aware of it."

"How have things been with you guys?"

"I've only been texting him since I got back. He's been trying to talk on the phone, but I'm trying to keep some boundaries and protect my heart."

"I think you're fighting a losing battle."

"How so?"

"Because you're too late to protect your heart. You're already head over heels for him and it's not going to go away."

"Oh God." I bury my face in my hands. "I can't believe you're right. What should I do?"

"Whatever you want. If you want things to work out with Clancy, then you can't freeze him out. He's probably trying to give you space. Be careful, though, or you might drive him right into someone else's arms. Is that what you want?"

"No, not at all. It's the opposite of what I want."

"Just talk to him about your concerns. They're not going to go away by pretending they don't exist."

"Hey, how are you?"

"I'm good. How are you two doing?" His deep voice wraps around me like a hug. Why haven't I called him sooner?

"We're good. She's growing every day. I think I'm much bigger than when you saw me last."

"Wow. It's only been a week."

"Right? I think she's going to be a hockey player."

"Well that goes without saying, but why do you think so?"

"She beats me up. She's always kicking and punching. Maybe she wants to be a martial artist."

"There's plenty of fighting in hockey." He chuckles.

"Have you guys come down from the Beanpot high yet?"

"Oh, for sure. Coach gave us one day to screw around, and since then I think he's been more relentless. He doesn't want our egos getting too big."

"Too late," I tease.

"Hey. Be nice."

"The truth hurts."

"How's school going? Is it too much for you?"

"No, it's good. I'm doing well in all of my classes. I am looking forward to being done for the summer. It will be good with Molly to have time to adjust."

"Are you really planning on returning to school in September?"

"I'm going to try like hell. It will depend on a lot of other factors."

"Like what?"

"How she's sleeping. Who can watch her. If my parents will still pay."

"Would they withhold the money because of Molly?"

"Not withhold as much as they might want me to take the year off and be with the baby."

"Maybe you'll want that too."

"I might. It's hard to say because I'm not in that situation now and never have been. I don't know how much work it's going to be to have a newborn. I've been reading books trying to learn everything I need to know."

"My mom gave me a book to read on pregnancy and what to expect after the baby comes."

"Have you even opened it?" I scoff. I bet he's been too busy hugging other girls.

"I finished reading it."

"When did she give it to you?"

"After I dropped you at the airport. I had to go to my mom's shop and help her with the inner city kids' class. She gave it to me then."

"And you already blew through it. I'm impressed."

"Do you have any questions for me, because I know more than I want to about what's going on in your body. If you give birth vaginally, I can't look. I don't ever want to see your beautiful pussy stretched out like that."

"Oh my God." I snort. "I don't even want to think about that part. I try to avoid the actual birthing when I think about having the baby. It's like one minute she's in my stomach and the next she's in my arms. I'm skipping all the gross details."

"One of the most disgusting things to me is the mucus plug."

"What is that? I don't even know about that."

"It's a barrier that seals your cervix during pregnancy. That and the amniotic sac help to protect the baby."

"Where and when does this plug go?" I can't believe he's telling me something I didn't know.

"Your mucus plug falls out when you get closer to delivering the baby. It's a sign that your cervix is softening and opening."

"I can't wait," I droll.

He chuckles. "It's a good thing. It means the pregnancy is almost over."

"I guess that's the only positive way of looking at mucus falling out of my vagina."

"If you have any more questions about the rest of your pregnancy, I'm your man."

If only he was. "Good to know."

"Can we talk about why you've been avoiding me?" His question surprises me and I'm not ready for it. I figured he'd ask me right away, not after we'd been talking for a bit.

"I don't really have a concrete reason. I guess I just don't want you to feel obligated to change your life. You seemed so happy with all your friends around you that night at the party."

"I was happy. We'd just won the championship. But you being there made it more special. Most of the people who were there could've left and I wouldn't have even noticed. But when you went upstairs, I felt your absence."

"I'm sorry. I just felt like the annoying baby momma. I didn't want to be your buzz kill, keeping you from all your adoring fans."

"Do you mean female fans?" He sounds amused and it angers me.

"What if I do?" I snip back.

"Nothing. I think you should know by now that I'm not interested in anyone but you."

"How would I know that, Clancy, when girls were plastering themselves to the front of your body and you were going along with it?"

"They were?"

"Are you being deliberately obtuse?"

"No, I'm really not. I have girls hug me and I think nothing of it because I'm not interested in them."

"Well, from where I was sitting it looked like you thought it was great."

"I barely remember to be honest. I guess I'll have to be more mindful."

"But that's what I'm getting at. I don't want you to change

who you are because I'm having your baby. Being a good father has nothing to do with you hugging other girls. And we weren't supposed to be more than a one-night hookup anyway."

"I'm not sure what you're saying. Do you want me to date other girls? Or do you want me not to? Because you complained I was hugging them, but now it seems like you're saying it's okay."

"I'm making a point."

"What point?" He sighs and I picture him thrusting his hand through his hair in frustration.

"Be whomever you want to be. If you want to be with other girls, then be with them."

"If you think I'm going to tell you to be with another guy, you're crazy."

"Not while I'm pregnant, silly." The silence grows until I can't bear it any longer. "I'll let you go. I'm sure you have things to do."

"Yeah, I've got big plans tonight. Women to hug and beers to drink." He laughs.

"Don't be an asshole."

"But you told me to be who I wanted to be."

I disconnect the call and start to cry. Somewhere along the way, that conversation went from awesome to completely off the rails and I think it's my fault. Stupid hormones. I can't even think things through logically anymore. I wish I could sleep for the next seven weeks and wake up once the baby is here.

CHAPTER TWENTY-FOUR

Clancy

Dropping my phone on my bed, I fall to my back on the mattress. What the hell was that all about? Pregnancy really does make women crazy. More crazy than they already can be - completely certifiable. I can't even wrap my brain around the logic she used. I guess I better chalk it up to hormones and hope she sticks to texting for now.

Damn. Being so far away from her is depressing. If we were in the same state, I'd go over to her apartment and console her. I'd ease any fears she has and make her see how much I care about her. Hell, I might even be in love with her. Who am I kidding? I'm completely gone for her. I haven't looked at another woman in over seven months. *Seven months.* That's unheard of for me. She knows this and she's still riding the crazy train. *Women.*

March has roared in like a lion, as the saying goes. And the lion keeps roaring. Almost three weeks in and we're still getting buried under snow. Everyone's in a miserable mood because of it. Winters in Massachusetts are tough, and when they drag on well into March, it puts everyone on edge.

Tenley and I have settled into a pattern of a brief text or two each night for the past two weeks. We haven't spoken since our last call. I think she's embarrassed about her bizarre behavior and I don't want to deal with her hormones. I feel guilty for not calling her. And for taking the easy way out. She deserves better. Tomorrow I'm going to be a better man and dial her up.

Have I been being an asshole by not making the effort? Possibly.

But what guy wants to get yelled at by his woman?

And the kicker is, she's not even my woman, yet.

With eight weeks left in her pregnancy, I know I need to bridge the giant gap that's erupted between us. In her mind, I'm fucking five different girls and partying every night.

When in reality I've been practicing extra for hockey and spending more time in the gym. With my dream of playing professional hockey so close to coming true, I can't let it get away from me.

"Dude, you look like shit," Owen tells me.

"Thanks."

"Seriously. What's going on with you?"

"I've been training like a fiend and not sleeping well." I don't want to explain how I miss Tenley in my bed. I've never been one to spend the night with a girl, but all it took was three nights with her and I can't sleep well without her.

"How's Tenley doing?"

"She says everything's good."

"You sound like you're not sure."

"We haven't been talking. We're only sharing texts now."

"Why?"

"She got weird on me and hung up during our last conversation. And ever since she only texts."

"So, why don't you call her?"

I run my palm across my aching forehead. "Because I'm an asshole."

"What does you being an asshole have to do with it?"

"You're not going to disagree?" One corner of my lips arc upward in a crooked smile.

"There's nothing to disagree with. You're a huge asshole. But you're still a great guy and I know you're not the type to treat a woman badly. Especially one you care about."

"Love. I think I love her."

"Wow. No wonder you look like shit. Are you quaking in your boots with fear?"

"Ha, I might be. How do I know for sure if it's love? I've never felt this way about anyone, so I have nothing to gauge it by."

"Do you think about her more than anything else? I mean thinking about her to the point of distraction."

"Yep. I can't concentrate. Everytime I try to I focus on what I'm doing, she slips into my thoughts and takes over."

"Do you worry about her when you're not with her?"

"Yes, and that's why I'm an asshole for not calling. I've been worrying non-stop and she has no idea."

"We all do stupid things in the name of love. And dealing with a pregnant woman is no easy feat. I feel for you because you guys have started your relationship while she's pregnant. You've grown to love her during this pregnancy." He grins. "But on a positive note, if you can love her while she's pregnant, you can love her forever. It sounds ridiculous, but I swear it's true." We both laugh.

"Tenley was easy to fall for. There's so much to love about her. I don't really think I had a choice."

"Yeah, Eliza definitely knocked me off my feet. I wasn't expecting her."

"How is she doing? Is she feeling okay?"

"She's doing surprisingly well. I'm overwhelmed with all the doctor appointments and the exorbitant amount of information we're fed each visit."

"Have you learned about an episiotomy yet?"

"No. It sounds painful. What is it?"

"Oh, it's painful for sure. It's a surgical incision of the perineum, which is basically the taint."

"What?" His expression is one of disgust.

"They do it to quickly enlarge the opening, so the baby can pass through."

"Oh Jesus. I'm not watching. I'm going to keep my eyes on Eliza's face the entire time."

"Right? I'm going to do the same. Giving birth is like something out of a horror movie."

"How do you know this shit?"

"I'm reading books about pregnancy and childbirth."

"Wow. Good for you, man. You're not that much of an asshole then. I haven't read anything yet."

"I can't go to her appointments with her. And I can't make her regurgitate all the details every time she has one."

"What else do I need to know about?"

"After the baby is born they get their periods for like a month."

"Get the fuck out."

"I'm not kidding."

"Christ. A handful of days each month is enough. How are we supposed to handle a month?"

"And women say it's a man's world. I watched a video of a c-section."

"Why?"

"I'm trying to be prepared in case she has to have one."

"Was it as bad as I imagine?"

"It's worse. Do yourself a favor and don't watch. If Eliza has one, there's a drape that will block the view of what they're doing. You don't have to watch. Unless you want to see what her guts look like."

"Fuck no. I'll be scarred for life."

"Here's how I look at it. Mothers give birth and go through all this stuff and they forget about it. They must right? If they didn't, they'd never have another kid. Every family in the world would be one child only."

"That makes sense."

"But the problem is, guys don't forget. How can we if we have to watch all this shit?"

"What are you saying? That women are lucky because they can forget how horrific it all is?"

"That's exactly what I'm saying."

"Hey, Mom." I lean over and kiss her cheek.

"Hi, honey. How's everything?" She gives me a quick hug and then looks me over.

"Good. The roads are shit. Are we still having class?"

"Yes. It started too late to cancel. And those kids look forward to this too much to shut down."

"If you need a ride home later, I can take you."

"I'll be fine. Why do you look so glum?"

"Too much on my mind, I guess."

"What are you so worried about?"

"Do you think I'll be a good father?"

"Oh, honey. I think you'll be a wonderful father."

"How do you know?"

"I've watched you work with kids for three years now. You're more of a father figure to some of them than anyone in their lives."

"But it's different when it's your kid and you have to be there all the time."

"That's true, but you'll take it in stride like you do everything else in life."

"I don't want to be a part-time dad and only see my daughter once a month."

"Then don't be."

"You make it sound so easy."

"It kind of is. As I see it, there are a couple of ways you can be a full-time parent. The first is, you'll have to move down to Virginia to be near Tenley and Molly. And the second is, you can take a chance and tell Tenley how you feel about her."

"What if she doesn't love me? Or even like me?"

"She loves you. I could see it in the way she looked at you. No woman looks at a man like that unless they feel strongly about them."

"What if she doesn't want to come with me wherever I end up?"

"Maybe you should start talking about this stuff with her soon, so you're prepared either way. There may come a point where you have to make some tough decisions you won't want to."

"I can't give up my dream, Mom."

"Hopefully, you won't have to, but remember, sometimes dreams change."

We move about setting up for the group of inner city kids who come to my mom's shop every week to paint pottery. We place bowls of water in front of each seat and cans of brushes in the middle of the tables. The kids start filing in one at a time. They hang their coats up on the hooks at the back of the room and collect their projects they've been working on.

Bobby, one of my mother's longest running students, is painting a motorcycle and doing a bang up job at it.

"Hey, that's looking pretty sweet. You're doing a great job on the small details."

"Someday I'm going to have a bike just like this."

"What's your favorite motorcycle?"

"The Road King."

"What color would you choose?"

"This blue." He points to the paint he's using. It's an electric blue.

"Nice. Do you know anyone with a Harley?"

"Nah. No one in my neighborhood has the money for a bike."

It's heartbreaking how Bobby is aware of this already and he's only twelve. It has me thinking about what else he's aware of that he doesn't need to be at his young age.

"You can be the first one to have a bike. You can be a role model for all the others."

He smiles, his eyes filled with hope as they connect with mine.

"Work hard and stay out of trouble, Bobby, and you can achieve great things."

"Like you?"

"I'm still a work in progress, Bobby, but I'm working hard and staying out of trouble for sure. We'll see how it goes for me."

"I hope you make the NHL. I want to tell all my friends I know someone famous."

"Ha. If I make it, I'm bringing you to a game."

"You promise, Clancy?"

"Absolutely, bud. Will you be my biggest fan?"

"You know it." He grins widely.

"Keep up the good work." I give him a nod and move on

to check out how the rest of the kids are doing. I offer help or encouragement, depending on what's needed.

When the class time's up, they help me clean up and place their projects in the back room on the shelf. They grab their jackets and some are reluctant to put them on. I wish they didn't have to return to whatever home situations are making them drag their feet.

Standing at the door, I hold my hand out for a high five from each of them as they walk out the door. It's part of our twice weekly routine.

When they're all gone, I close the door and turn to find my mom smiling.

"What are you so happy about?"

"You. I'm so proud of the man you've grown up to be. If you still have concerns about what kind of father you'll be, think about how wonderful you are with each one of those kids. You make each of them feel special in some way. That's a talent that not everyone has. Making someone else feel better about themselves or brightening their day is a gift."

"I know that, Mom, because you taught me. If you like the man I am, it's because of you. You're a great role model."

She cups her hands over her nose and mouth. "Oh." Her eyes fill with tears. "There you go making me feel special."

"You are special, Mom. I don't tell you often enough, so you better hear it now." We both laugh.

"Why don't you go home and call Tenley? She's the one you need to make feel special."

"You're right, I do. I haven't talked to her in too long and texting is too impersonal for someone I care so much about."

CHAPTER TWENTY-FIVE

Clancy

When I get home from my mom's shop, I immediately head up to my room to call Tenley. There's no answer, which is strange. She always answers when I call. Unless she's angry at me. If she is, I hope she gets over it because I really want to talk to her.

Sinking down into my recliner, I remove my boots and type out a text to Tenley.

Me: *Please call me. I need to talk to you.*

Pushing back, I raise the ottoman on the recliner and get comfortable. Closing my eyes, I wait for her to call.

The persistent ringing of my phone wakes me from a much needed nap. Glancing at the screen I notice it's Sophie calling.

"Hey, Soph."

"Clancy, Tenley's in the hospital."

"What happened?" Horrific images of a car accident assault my mind.

"She wasn't feeling well all day. She hasn't been sleeping well, so she insisted she was overtired."

"Soph, get to the point."

"She's in labor. They're going to take her in for an emergency c-section soon. Get on a flight."

My stomach sinks. "It's too early for the baby to be born."

"She's thirty-three weeks. There's a good survival rate at this age. Think positive."

"Fuck. I won't be able to get there for at least two or three hours. Will you keep me updated?"

"Of course."

I hang up without saying goodbye. I'm numb and having difficulty forming coherent thoughts. Why didn't I call her last night? Shit. Is she in labor early because she's been stressed out?

Is this somehow my fault? I won't be able to live with myself if this has anything to do with me not calling her.

I pull up the website for the airline, booking a flight that leaves in seventy minutes. I throw boxers, socks, jeans, and a couple of shirts in a backpack. I grab my phone charger, toothbrush, and toothpaste, and drop them in the bag before zipping it. I'm ready.

Running down the stairs, I stop in the doorway to the living room. "Oliver, can you take me to the airport?"

"Sure." He stands and skirts around the coffee table coming my way. "Everything okay?"

"Tenley is having the baby early and I need to get there ASAP."

Oliver shoves his feet into some boots and grabs his coat from the closet. "I'm ready."

We head out the door. "Let's take my truck. I'll drive and then you can bring it back."

"Whatever you want, man."

Of course the roads are slippery, and I need to keep my speed low. I also happen to hit every red light on the way to the highway. "Goddammit." I slam my palm down on the steering wheel.

"Clancy, it's going to be fine. Getting worked up isn't going to help Tenley or your daughter," Oliver reassures.

"I know. I just want to be there already. She's alone and scared. I should be with her." I can't imagine what Tenley is going through.

"You can't help that she went into labor early. Did the doctor think this would happen?"

"No. She had an appointment last week and everything was as it should be."

"See? All you can do is get on your flight and you'll be there before you know it."

I pull over to the side of the curb in front of the airline terminal that I'm taking. I hop out and grab my carry-on, slinging it over my shoulder. Oliver meets me at the back of the truck as he heads for the driver's seat.

"Call me and let me know what's going on."

"Thanks, man." We share a quick hug and then I'm on my way. Speed walking through the airport, I'm worried I'm going to be flagged for suspicious behavior and kept from my flight. I slow down a little. Getting detained won't help me get to Virginia faster.

I pass by the area where Tenley and I said our goodbyes less than three weeks ago. I'm through the metal detectors without a hitch and heading toward the gate with twenty minutes to spare.

While I wait to get on the plane, I text my mom and let her know what's going on. I also drop Cassie a text to see if there's any news about Tenley.

Cassie: *No updates. Still waiting to hear what's going on.*

Her reply doesn't have me feeling very hopeful. God, please let our baby and Tenley be okay. I'm so concerned that my stomach is nauseous and my knee is bouncing up and down while I wait for my seat section to be called to the plane.

The hour-long flight is spent with images of Tenley playing on a non-stop loop in my head. I see her standing at the bar the night of the wedding, looking more beautiful than any woman I'd ever set eyes on. God, how I wanted her that night.

We land and taxi to the terminal. Once I'm off the plane, it only takes me ten minutes until I'm in a taxi headed for the hospital. I pray all the way there, begging for Tenley and my baby to be okay. I want to be able to hold them both and tell them how much I love them.

When the taxi stops in front of Fairfax Inova hospital in Falls Church, I throw money at the driver and shoot out the back door.

Hurrying into the front entrance, I search the map on the wall to find the maternity unit. I take the appropriate elevator up to the third floor and hurry to the nurses' station.

"I'm looking for Tenley Davenport."

"And you are?"

"Her fiance." The words come out naturally. I don't even think about it first. But it's probably for the best. I want to make sure I can see her. "She may be giving birth to our daughter right now."

"She's in room 328. Follow this hallway and take a right at the end."

"Thank you," I call out as I'm already en route to her room. Once I round the corner at the end of the hallway, hers is the first room on the left. Peeking inside, I see Tenley asleep in the bed.

Quietly, I maneuver around her bed, placing my bag on the window ledge. When I turn around, I find her watching me.

"Hey," I say, smiling. Leaning over the side railing, I press a kiss on her forehead. I fight back tears of relief, dragging a deep breath in through my nose.

"Hi," she whispers.

"How are you?"

"I'm still breathing."

"I'm glad to hear it. How's the baby?" Now that I've asked, I'm afraid of what the answer might be.

"She's okay. They've got her in the NICU, but they said her vitals are strong. She was a good size for how early she is."

"What's the NICU?"

"It's the neonatal intensive care unit."

"Are you sure she's okay?" My heartbeat kicks up, thundering behind my rib cage.

"She's fine."

"What did she weigh?"

"Five pounds two ounces, and she's twenty inches long."

I beam. "Thank God she's okay. I was so worried about both of you."

Tenley's eyelids keep falling shut and then snapping open. She needs to sleep. "I'm going to go see our little girl. Take a nap, babe. I'll make sure she's okay."

"Thank you."

"You don't have to thank me. I'm so relieved my girls are both okay."

"I'm glad you're here."

"There's nowhere else I'd be. Do I need to call anyone for you?"

"No, my parents and Cassie are getting something to eat. They'll be back later."

I find the NICU and the nurse in charge makes me show her ID before she'll speak to me. Apparently, I was supposed to be issued a bracelet that has Molly's information on it. But I came in like a hurricane and rushed off to see Tenley.

The nurse hands me a gown that I pull on over my clothes and instructs me to clean my hands with foam sanitizer before she'll hand Molly over to me. Making a cradle of my arms, I hold my breath as she transfers her over. Wrapped up like a little pink burrito, she's warm and surprisingly solid. I make sure to support her neck like all the books I read suggested.

Lowering into a rocking chair, I stare down at my daughter. *My daughter.* The most incredible words. God, she's beautiful. The blonde fuzz on her head is soft and downy like peach fuzz. Her tiny nose is just like her mom's and so is the stubborn set of her little chin. I can't take my eyes off her. She's a miracle in more ways than one. All I can do is beam down at her. She already holds my heart firmly in her tiny little hand and I never want her to let it go.

It's impossible to describe the magnitude of love I'm experiencing. Tears of joy spill down my cheeks without me realizing it. There's a pleasant ache in the middle of my chest with her name on it. My life is forever changed because of this miniscule little girl.

"Molly, your daddy loves you so much. You're my little fighter." She grabs my pinky finger with her tiny fingers, holding on to me so trustingly. My heart squeezes in reaction." Don't." I pause, choked up, swallowing past the lump in my throat. "Don't tell Mommy, but I'm going to teach you how to play hockey someday, and you're going to love it."

I sit there rocking her for so long my ass feels like it's asleep, and yet I still keep rocking.

"I thought I'd find you here," Cassie calls out as she approaches.

"Isn't she beautiful?"

"Of course she is. How could she not be with you two for parents?"

"Where are Mr. and Mrs. Davenport?"

"They said goodnight to Tenley and now they went home."

"I suppose you want a turn rocking this little angel?"

"Hell yes. Auntie needs a chance to hold her."

"Go get a gown and sanitize your hands and then I might let you have her."

"Yes, Dad. See, you're a natural, looking out for her already." She slides a gown on and foams her hands, rubbing them together as she walks toward us. "Why don't you go confess your love to Tenley while I hold Molly?"

"As long as she's awake, that's my plan."

"It's about damn time." She winks.

———

Tenley's awake when I sit beside her bed. "How do you feel?"

"I'm a little sore. The meds help, but they don't take the pain from the surgery away completely."

I take her hand and raise it to my lips. "I'm so sorry I wasn't here with you."

"How could you have been? It all happened so fast."

"Cassie's with Molly now. If you're not too tired, I'd like to hear how it all went down."

"No, I just woke up from a nice nap, so I'm good." She smiles sleepily and I'm not convinced she's fully rested. "As soon as I got here they put a monitor on me to check the baby's heartbeat and measure contractions. When her heartbeat got wonky, they told me they were going to do a c-section. I didn't realize how serious everything was until they rushed me off to surgery only moments later."

"Were you awake for her birth?"

"No. They knocked me out. There wasn't enough time to give me an epidural."

"Who was here with you?"

"Cassie drove me here and stayed with me until they took me away. My parents came while I was in surgery."

"Where's Sophie?"

"She was with Joey and Miles was working, so she couldn't leave. She said she'd get here as soon as she can."

"Have you seen our daughter yet?"

"I saw her when I was in recovery."

"She's perfect." I squeeze her hand.

"I think so too."

"Thank you."

"You had a hand in making her. I couldn't have done it without you."

"She wouldn't be here without you. Thank you for keeping her safe."

"We did it. We made a baby and she's here." Gratitude filled eyes stare up at me, making me feel like the king of the universe.

"I know she's barely out of the oven, so to speak, but where are you going when you leave here?"

"I guess my parents' house. The shower invitations weren't even sent out. I don't have any stuff for the baby yet."

"Leave everything to me."

"Yeah, sure." She rolls her eyes.

"I mean it. I'll take care of everything."

"It's going to be expensive. I don't have the crib or a dresser. Then again, I don't have any baby clothes to put in the dresser." She giggles about the predicament, reminding me of why I love her so much.

"I have money my grandparents gave me that I've never used. I can't think of anything better to spend some of it on than Molly."

"If you're sure."

"Absolutely. Is there anything you need?"

"No, I have everything I need." She squeezes my hand.

CHAPTER TWENTY-SIX

Clancy

"I'm so proud of you," Sophie hugs me. "I knew you'd be there for Tenley all the way."

"I'm so proud of you too," Miles jokes, shaking my hand.

"We need to get back to the house and relieve Miles' sister of her babysitting duties."

"Thank you for coming by and for everything you did to help Tenley during the pregnancy."

"Please. She's my best friend. That trumps being your cousin."

"I have no doubt that's true." I grin as I watch them step inside the elevator.

When I return to Tenley's room, she's nursing Molly. I always imagined I'd be put off by seeing her nursing, but I'm not. Tenley is naturally loving and nurturing. The two of them together is a sight I'll never tire of. It doesn't matter what they're doing, these two girls are the loves of my life.

"It's been a long day." I groan as I sit in the seat closest to Tenley.

"Oh, has it?" Tenley's eyes snap fire at me. "I feel for you."

There she is, my little spitfire. Even when she's just had surgery.

I laugh. "Touché. I'm not taking away from what you did, but I did travel seven states in an hour." I polish my nails on my shirt.

"Bully for you."

"On a more serious note, I want to apologize for not calling you the past two weeks."

"I didn't call you either."

"I know, but you were dealing with a lot and I should've been there for you."

"Did you really want to hear all my complaints? I could've told you how the mean girls at school called me fat or made snide comments about me being knocked up."

"No, I wouldn't have wanted to hear that because it would've angered me. And I'd have wanted to grab the next flight and tell those little shits off."

"That would've been a huge help," she says dryly. "Maybe it was for the best we didn't talk. Besides, everything is fine now, so what does it matter?"

"It matters to me. I was planning to call you tonight."

"Sure you were," she teases.

"I was going to tell you how much I care about you, but that's not really the truth."

"It's not?" She frowns, her skin pinching together between her brows.

"Nope." I lean forward, bracing my arms on the bed railing. "Things really do have a way of working out for the best, because I'm here with you."

"Are you going to tell me in person how you don't care about me?"

"I am. But only because I want you to know that I don't just care about you; I'm hopelessly, irrevocably in love with you."

"You are?" she whispers, her eyes glassy with tears.

"I am. Who knew our one night together would tie us together forever?"

"You did when you poked the hole in the condom." She giggles.

"Is that the way it happened?"

"Yep. You wanted me so badly, you decided you'd do anything to have me. At least that's the story I'm going with."

"Can I tell you the story I prefer?"

"Sure."

"I think we're two people who were meant to be together that got a helpful shove from the universe. With the physical distance between us, if we hadn't gotten pregnant, we may not have ended up together. And what a tragedy that would've been. I can't imagine spending a single day without both of you in my world."

"I love you, Clancy Wilde."

"I love you more. Does this finally mean I get to see what you wrote in your diary about me?"

Tenley and Molly were released from the hospital, at the same time, four days after her birth. I ordered everything she needed online and set it all up in the spare bedroom at her parents' house.

I had to return to Boston for the semifinals of the Hockey East tournament. We're playing Harvard and we've been neck and neck for the whole game. We're in sudden-death, five minute overtime, now and we can't seem to shake their defense. They're on us like flies to garbage. Just when I think we're going to hold them off and get a chance at a goal for the win, the puck is tipped inside our net. Fuck. And just like that, one goal put an end to our season.

Oliver pats me on the back. "Good game, bro."

"Not as good as we'd have liked, though."

"Hey, Wilde," Ben Jackson, one of the Harvard players calls my name. "Congratulations on your daughter. Hope she doesn't mind having a loser for a dad."

Already frustrated at our loss, his words anger me. I clench my teeth.

"Ignore him," Oliver cautions.

"I knew you were a pussy," Ben shouts.

Shit talking time has now officially ended.

I go after him, shaking off my gloves and circling in close. "Guess it's time to find out."

I grab his shirt collar with my left hand and begin firing off right hooks as fast as I can. He does exactly the same and we find ourselves spinning in a circle at center ice, locked in a real life game of Rock 'em Sock 'em Robots.

The fans quickly stop filtering out toward the arena exits and begin cheering and jeering us on. In my periphery I see Oliver circling around us looking to throw hands, but no one steps up.

Ducking my head as his punches come in, he ends up hitting the top of my helmet. It isn't long before his hand begins throbbing and his punches slow.

I mix in a few uppercuts and seconds later his knees buckle. He slumps to the ice and the refs skate in to make sure it's over.

"Who's the pussy now?" I spit on the ice next to him and skate away. Oliver meets me on my way to the boards roaring with laughter. "That's one way to end the season."

"She loves her daddy," Tenley sinks down next to me on the couch, leaning her head on my shoulder.

"That's no surprise. She's a female and women love me. In fact, chicks have been digging me my whole life." I wink.

"Pfft. I could say the same about guys."

"Guys dig me too," I joke.

"Haha, funny man. I meant me."

"Let's not talk about which guys want you. It will only anger me. It still burns my ass how Harry was looking at you that night at the party."

"That was months ago."

"It doesn't matter how long it's been."

"Wait. How was he looking at me?"

I raise a brow as I look down into her mischievous eyes. "Like a man who wants his ass kicked."

"Are all Boston boys as touchy as you?"

"It's not touchy; it's protective. I take care of what's mine."

"And I'm yours?"

"Fuck yes, you're mine. You're not one of those women who's going to say they don't belong to anyone but yourself are you? Because it's way too late for that, babe. I'm a possessive asshole. It's who I am and I don't see it changing."

"Nope. I like your barbarian ways."

Leaning over, I capture her lips in a brief kiss. When I pull back she frowns. "I want more too, but not in your parents' house," I explain. She just got out of the hospital earlier this week. We have six weeks to wait too before we can have sex. Which wouldn't be that long, but we've been waiting for seven and a half months already. But what's a little longer when it's waiting for the girl of my dreams?

"Ugh. I know. And it's going to be like this indefinitely."

"I'm not so sure about that. I have to ask you something and I want you to be completely honest with me. If I got selected by the Bruins would you and Molly move to Boston and live with me? I'll do whatever I have to in order to spend everyday with you guys. You're the ones who matter most."

"Of course we would."

"What about school?"

"What about it?"

"You're a senior. Wouldn't you want to finish your degree at King?"

"You're more important than what school I get my degree from. I'd just meet with my advisor and see if there's a way to do the rest online. Worst case, I take a semester off and finish out at one of the many awesome colleges in Boston."

"Just like that?"

"Yep. Exactly like that."

"Then I have something to show you." I grab my phone and pull up the press release from the Bruins.

Clancy Wilde, Boston University, has agreed to terms with the Boston Bruins.

Wilde has agreed to terms for a two-year, entry-level contract with the Bruins that will begin for the upcoming season.

Wilde turns 23 on July 24. He was undrafted the past two seasons and became eligible for free agency this year. He attended camps with both the Bruins and Flyers last summer.

Wilde was captain of the Terriers team for two years. Their season came to an end with a 3-2 loss to Harvard in the semifinals of the Hockey East tournament.

"Wilde is the hardest worker I've ever had the privilege to coach. He's relentless in his training and his work ethic. His positive outlook is unmatched. He can turn a bad situation into a productive one and motivate the rest of his teammates with a few words." - Boston University coach, Dave Cutter

Tenley's crying by the time she finishes reading the release that went out earlier today. "You got an offer?"

I nod. "They met with me when I was in Boston, and I signed the paperwork."

"I'm so proud of you. After everything you had weighing on your mind this year, you still achieved your goal. You made it happen just like you planned all along."

"It wasn't as easy as that. This was my last chance. I didn't get selected the last two years. It was a make it or break it time for me."

"Well, you made it. I'm so freaking proud of you. My baby daddy is a Boston Bruin." She beams. "When are we moving?"

CHAPTER TWENTY-SEVEN

Tenley

TWO MONTHS LATER

"Keep your eyes closed for one sec. I'm almost ready." I hear a key turning in the lock and I smile. "Okay, babe. Are you ready to see our new home?"

"I don't know. Am I?" I entrusted Clancy with obtaining and decorating our new apartment. In a brownstone in Brookline, the rent is astronomical, but the area is safe.

"Have a little faith, babe. I have great taste. I picked you, didn't I?"

"That's true."

"Open your eyes," he orders.

My eyelids raise and I gasp. He closes the door behind me as I take in all the details. The dark hardwoods gleam throughout the open space. There's a beige area rug in front of the large, brown leather sectional, and a rustic coffee table with my favorite books stacked on it.

Molly looks out from her car seat, glancing inquisitively around. At two months of age, she's already curious about everything. "Go ahead, babe. Check out the kitchen," Clancy encourages.

I move through the living room and over to the enormous granite island. The metal barstools are painted black and the seats are round in shape. I sink down on one, spinning around. "Whee," I call out as I turn.

"I knew you'd like those." Clancy chuckles.

Rising, I maneuver around the island, standing behind it, leaving Clancy on the other side. Leaning forward, I place my arms on the granite and giving him a clear view down my tank top. "What can I get for you?" I ask in a husky voice.

"Be careful or you're going to find yourself trying out the new bed in ways you weren't expecting. You'll get a clear view of the ceiling and nothing else."

"Don't tease me," I retort.

He grips my arm with one hand and carries Molly's seat with his other. Placing her down in the hallway outside our bedroom door, he stalks me like a wild animal. My pulse races with lust as the blood thrums through my veins.

He pushes me and I tumble backward on the king sized bed. The gray and black comforter is soft beneath me. Placing a knee on the mattress, he crawls between my legs.

Bracing his upper body with one arm, the fingers on his other hand trace out the shape of my cheek. "You're so fucking beautiful. Are we really going to do this?"

"Oh God. Yes, please. I want you so bad."

"It's been too long since I've been inside you." He brushes his nose along the side of mine while his fingers dexterously undo my shorts. He has them down my legs in seconds. My pulse kicks up another notch along with my breathing. I've never been so turned on in my life. The only time that even comes close to comparing is the first night we were together. It's hard to believe it's nine and a half months later and this is only the second time we're about to have sex.

My hands push on his chest, urging him back. "Get undressed."

He kneels between my legs tearing his t-shirt over his head. I raise my torso and tug my tank top off. Reaching behind me, I remove my bra while he scrambles out of his shorts and boxer briefs. He slides down between my spread legs once more and I moan as our bare skin comes into contact.

"Christ. I might come before I get inside you. Your skin is so fucking soft, and your curves..." His jaw tenses. "Jesus. I've never seen anything sexier in my life." He clasps each of my hands, raising them over my head. "As much as I want to fuck you hard and fast, I'd rather make love to you."

"You can do whatever you want with me. But for fuck sake just do *something*. I'm dying."

He drags his cock through my slit, sliding back and forth over my clit.

"Oh," I gasp. He keeps up the to and fro motion, the head of his cock teasing my clit until it's swollen and as needy as me. I'm on the verge of coming when his lips fasten over mine. His tongue strokes and teases as his hips move faster.

Soft strands of his hair fall around us as we kiss, trailing over my skin in a sensual caress. One more urgent stroke over my clit and I fall, every inch of me trembling and quivering.

Clancy thrusts into me with a deep groan. "Oh fuck." His first strokes are long and slow, but he picks up the pace with my heels on his lower back driving him on. His hands release their hold on mine.

My fingers sink into his thick locks, exposing his face. The shades of gold, green, and brown in his irises are magnified with passion. I've never felt more connected to him. "Take me. I'm yours."

He growls in agreement and clasps the back of my thigh with an iron hard grip. Our bodies slapping together, his hips move impossibly fast until he finds his release. He strokes a few more times before collapsing on top of me. His lips nuzzle my neck as my hands stroke down his back soothingly. Our harsh breaths break the silence.

He raises his head. "We can't wait so long for sex anymore. That orgasm was so powerful, I think it took five years off my life."

I laugh. "I'm all for not waiting."

"We didn't use a condom. Are you sure we're okay?"

"We did use one last time and it didn't matter."

"Are we good or should I start worrying now?"

"We should be fine; I'm on the pill. We even waited an extra two weeks just to be sure."

"Oh thank God. Don't get me wrong, I love Molly, but one is good for now."

Raising my head, I peek over at her in the hallway. She's sound asleep. Fortunately for us, she's been a great sleeper from the start.

He rolls to the side, pulling me onto his chest. "So what do you think of our bedroom?"

I giggle. "The bed's comfortable and the ceiling is extremely white. I like the way the comforter feels on my back."

"You can see how it feels on your knees next." He smirks.

"You did a great job choosing this place. I love it already."

"I'm glad. I want you to be happy here. I know it's going to be difficult being away from your family and friends."

"I have you and Molly. What more do I need? And Sophie and Cassie promised to visit this summer."

"Should we try out the shower and see if we can both fit comfortably?"

"I'm game."

After Molly woke up it was time for her to nurse. This kid can eat. She has her daddy's appetite. Once she's done, I hand her off to Clancy and he gently burps her as I right my clothing.

"I have the best part of this place to show you still."

"Is there a pool on the roof?" I perk up at the possibility.

"No. How would that be possible? It's not a flat roof."

"Damn. That's right. What's the surprise? It better be good to beat the pool I'm not getting."

"It's something we need more than a pool." He tugs me from the couch to my feet and we walk side by side with Clancy pointing the way. He pauses outside the door next to our room. "Are you ready?" His excitement is almost palpable as he turns the knob. "Behold, Princess Molly's room."

"Oh, Clancy, it's beautiful." Molly's bedroom walls have been painted with a castle and a forest scene. There are horses and a carriage too. "Did your mom do all this?"

He nods. "She did. She wanted her to have a fairytale room."

"It's perfect. What girl wouldn't love this room?"

"When she's old enough, we can tell her about our fairy-tale. How we met and ended up together," Clancy cuddles Molly, rubbing her back. She looks miniscule against his wide chest.

"We'll have to make up a G-rated version and save the X-rated one for when she's over thirty," I offer. "And we tell her if she has a goal, she can achieve it with focus and hard work. You're the perfect example of this. Your dream was to play professional hockey and you are."

"She needs to know that sometimes dreams change. Or you can have more than one. You're the perfect example of that."

"How so?" He takes my hand, drawing me in front of him. The three of us standing together.

"Hockey was my dream until you and I got together. And then you became part of my dream too. The most important part. I can live without hockey, but you know what I can't live without?"

"No."

He draws me against his chest, one arm holding me and one cradling Molly. "This. Our little family. I can't live without *us*."

"You'll never have to."

EPILOGUE

Clancy

FOUR YEARS LATER

Tenley leans her head on my shoulder. "Oh Clancy, it's perfect."

My eyes scan every square inch of the sun drenched warehouse space, taking in all the carefully planned out details. Wide windows let in natural light. Long, rectangular tables with benches on either side are spread throughout the main area and there are deep, wall to wall shelves at the end of the room where my mother can place all the active painting projects. The unpainted pottery will go in one of the back rooms, along with three specialty art classrooms. One will be for pottery making, another for painting on canvas and the final one will be for small woodworking projects.

"Daddy, can I paint something?" Molly places her tiny hands on my cheeks, turning my face to hers. Blue eyes so like her mother's stare into mine. Pretty soon she'll be too independent to let me carry her like this.

"Not now sweetie. You need to wait until the grand opening starts and then you can paint with grammy. She'll be teaching everyone how to make pretty things just like she does with you."

"When's that going to be?"

"In a few hours."

"Molly, why don't you come with me. You can help me finish setting everything up," my mom calls out as she adjust the position of one bench.

"Okay," she nods, a smile gracing her adorable little face. Pressing a kiss to her pert, freckled nose, I set her down on her feet. Tenley and I watch as she skips over to my mom. Her blonde curls bouncing all the way.

"She's growing like a little weed. What are we going to do?" Tenley whispers.

I turn to answer my wife and pause. Enraptured by her beauty I can only stare and marvel that she's mine. *How did I get so fucking lucky?*

I've spent many hours thinking about that question. How does one guy get blessed with so much good in his life? I'm married to the woman of my dreams. We have a precocious, healthy daughter. I'm still playing for the Bruins. The list could go on and on.

After my initial contract was up, the team renewed it for four more years offering me more money than I hoped. As a result of all the hard work I put in over the years, I have product endorsements making me millions of dollars. I get to play a game I love for my full-time job and at night I come home to the two people I love most.

When I was still in college, I promised myself if I was ever in a position to help the less fortunate, I would. That's what this grand opening today is all about. Wilde World of Art is a place where inner city kids who have no other after school programs available, can come and learn free of cost. My mom is in charge of running the program. She hired someone to manage the store at the old location because there are many loyal customers and she didn't want them to have to relocate to the new one.

But this is her baby and her input was the most influential in the design of this space. We repurposed an old warehouse and now she has plenty of room and even some on the second floor to expand if she needs to.

We did the grand opening up right including a ribbon cutting ceremony. I held up Molly so she could watch as her grandmother cut the red ribbon. She clapped and cheered as loud as she could and now she's busy painting with her grandmother.

"Clancy," my name is called out in a deep voice.

Pivoting around I find Bobby one of my favorite pottery students. I grin as I look him over. Tall and strong, he's growing into a fine young man. "Bobby, how are you?" I shake his hand, tugging him in for a quick hug.

"I'm good, man. Tenley, how are you?" He steps forward for a hug. Tenley has gotten to know Bobby from helping out my mom. She's come to care for him as much as I have.

"Bobby, I can't believe how much you've grown since I last saw you. What have you been eating?" Tenley asks.

He laughs. "I eat and work out a lot. I've been following the training program Clancy gave me."

I pat him on the back. "That's what I like to hear."

"This place looks sick. Your mom must be excited."

"She is. Are you?"

"Definitely."

"My mom and I were talking and we decided that we'd like you to work here. What do you think about that idea? You need a job, right?"

"Yes, sir. I'd love that."

"In addition to being paid hourly, you're going to get a full scholarship to whatever college you get accepted at."

"For real?" Bobby questions with his eyes open wider than I've ever seen.

"Yes, for real. I want you to keep focused and stay out of trouble. Can you do that?"

"You bet I can."

"Four years ago, I made you a promise that I'd never forget you and I haven't."

"And I made you a promise to work hard and stay out of trouble and I'm doing it."

"Keep it up and you'll have that Road King you've always wanted in no time."

Tenley settles on my chest, resting her chin on her arms. She stares up at me. "Today was a big success. Your mom must've been thrilled with the turnout."

"She was. She's excited to get a whole bunch of new students in there and so am I." My fingers trail through her dark tresses. The soft strands are like silk on my skin.

"Maybe you can get some of your friends from the team to help out once in a while."

"It's already taken care of. I've got a few of the guys on the schedule. One or two of them are even willing to come in weekly."

"Do you ever think about having another baby?" she questions, changing the subject. Her fingertips skim over my chest.

"I guess. I remember how adorable Molly was as a newborn, but it's so much work. Are you sure you want to start all over again?"

"Molly's four now. Even if I got pregnant tonight, she'd be

five when the baby was born. That's a big age difference between kids."

"You really want to go back to all those sleepless nights?"

"Plenty of our nights are sleepless now."

I wiggle my eyebrows. "Yeah, but for a different reason. And you've gotta admit you love it when I keep you up all night."

"I can't deny it. I have a confession to make."

"Is it a dirty one?"

"No." she laughs.

"Damn. Why can't it be a dirty one?"

She rolls her eyes. "I went off the pill. If you want to try for a baby now my womb is ripe."

"Jesus. Promise me you'll never say the words womb and ripe again in a sentence together." I shiver in disgust. "If you want another child, me and my boys are happy to help out. In fact, I bet I can get the job done in one shot." I wink.

She walks her fingers down my chest and over my stomach until she grabs me through my boxer briefs. "Think your stick can get the puck in the goal?"

I grin. "Every fucking time."

<hr>

Enjoy CHECKED?

Want to know more about Clancy's Football playing friends. Read the COMPLETE Boston Terriers Football Series TODAY.

PENALTY | DRIVE | COACH | TACKLE | JOCK | SCORE

<hr>

Want to find out how Sophie and Miles found their Happy Ever After?

Read about their Student/Teacher Romance in DEPRAVITY, book one of the King University Series.

ACKNOWLEDGMENTS

Thank you to every reader who purchased, borrowed or read CHECKED with Kindle Unlimited.

This books was challenging to write because of all the pregnancy details that I needed to research. Thank you to Andrea for all your help with the medical parts.

Thank you to my PA Diane for all the things you do to keep me organized and get my books seen. You went above and beyond for CHECKED. I'm so grateful to have you and your reminders that keep me on task.

I have to thank my amazing editor, Shauna Stevenson from Ink Machine Editing. You're so great about fitting me in when I need you to. I really appreciate how flexible you are and how quickly you work. Thank you for being so encouraging and for taking great care with my books.

Thank you to my proofreader Jodi Prellwitz Duggan. Thank you for fitting me in and doing a great job.

Marley Valentine, thank you for doing such a great job on the formatting. You always make my books look great. Thank you for also being such a great beta reader. Your feedback was helpful as always.

Thank you to Sam Keiffer for coming up with the last name Wilde for Clancy. It's the perfect choice.

Thank you to Monica Marti for educating me on the drink Devil's Advocate. It was a great choice for Tenley.

Thank you to all the members of my Facebook reader's group Spoiled by Chance for being so incredibly supportive of everything I write. You guys have embraced my storyline choices from day one. Thank you for all the shares you give my graphics and for recommending my books every chance you get. It's an amazing feeling to have such a strong support system behind me every step of the way.

ABOUT THE AUTHOR

Jacob Chance grew up in New England and still lives there today. He's a martial artist, a football fan, a practical joker and junk food lover.

All his books are available on **Amazon**

THE QUAKE SERIES

QUAKE | QUIVER | DELVE | TIED | DELUDE | QUAKE DUET | DELVE DUET

THE BOSTON TERRIERS SERIES

PENALTY | DRIVE | COACH | TACKLE | JOCK | SCORE

WORLD CLASS WRESTLING

TUSSLE | RUMBLE

KING UNIVERSITY SERIES

DEPRAVITY | DEVILRY | DEBAUCHERY

STANDALONES

PUNCHED | CANVAS | EDGE OF RETRIBUTION

FIND JACOB CHANCE

Amazon | Facebook | Twitter | Instagram | Goodreads | BookBub | Spoiled by Chance Reader's Group | Jacob's Newsletter

Made in United States
Orlando, FL
23 January 2022

13887159R00134